Shadows Falling

Kristin Cole

To my family, the best part of every day.

"There is no such thing as darkness; only a failure to see."

-Malcolm Muggeridge

Prologue

The year was not 2001 but it could have been. Walking up the winding path of St. Augustine's main campus, I felt the same, distinct sense of foreboding. The lush greenery yielded the same dread. The Tudor style brick buildings gave me the same feeling of panic. Taking in the campus as a whole, I had known then, just as now, the sheer burden of wealth and tradition that informed every inch of this sprawling landscape. And the same statement was sounding through my being, as it had eleven years earlier: I cannot do this. I cannot do this. I cannot do this.

I could not do this job. I could barely even manage this walk, with the tell-tale shoulder bag of the burdened teacher slamming into my aching leg. I had to lurch forward, while staring down at the cobbles, fearful of catching my cane in one of the picturesque cracks. I was Prufrock's scuttling crab. I was a misshapen Quasimodo, letting the bells toll. I was a 33 year old English teacher who had been struck by a car, walking home from this very campus, eight months earlier.

In 2001, I had been given this job that I knew I could not do, and I had done it. But standing here now, out of breath and feeling my tears gather behind my eyes, I knew I could not do it again. The pity was that I had to. September had come. As with the previous thirty Septembers, this month meant school. And I went to school. Short of national disasters, or the elusive fever, I was always in attendance. For the better part of these years I was happy to be so, but not any longer. I did not want to be here. There were too many shadows, too many reminders of how my life had changed.

Indeed the school had undergone seismic changes in the time that I was away; ironic, considering how immutable St. Augustine's had always seemed. Yet an influx of new faculty had to have some effect. I had no idea what, if anything, that meant for me. I had worked for over a decade to make my contributions valuable here, but when I was gone, other people contributed in ways that made me fear I had become redundant. My sudden hit and run accident had made me distrustful, almost expectant of darkness. I no longer felt at home here.

Wending my way to the campus' academic building, I welcomed some concentration on my physical self, painful though it was. My commute was mercifully short, but my right leg, now filled with what my doctor called hardware, felt worse in the car. I intended to walk to school, when I could.

If I did walk and utilized the alleyway which ran behind the athletic fields, my campus trek would be shorter than it was from the parking lot. St. Augustine's had once been the home of a group of horticultural monks; the grounds were spectacular but not organically best for a school. Buildings had been added to accommodate the growth beyond the two original dwellings and the pathways between them were rarely straight.

After briefly wondering if I should not first stop by the Towers, I turned left towards the academic building. Here, all classes, save special symposium, were held. The size of the building and student body also allowed for teacher's to have individual classrooms, though they were of irregular size and shape. My eleven year perch had been a second story room that overlooked the campus' front lawn. The radiators were loud and temperamental and the room had only one door, but I loved it. Bum leg or not, I was determined to keep my classroom, though grateful to have been offered the option to take one on the first floor. I intended to arrange it, as best I could, before the 10am General Faculty meeting.

St. Augustine possessed a Principal, in Sister Paul, who would schedule a meeting on Labor Day Monday and receive complete attendance from her faculty. It was easy enough to conclude that, had she wanted to see me prior to the meeting, such a directive would have been given. So I felt little guilt bypassing the Towers for now, knowing I would be returning there in approximately ninety minutes.

My classroom beckoned, though it also offered another brand of anxiety. I had not been there since closing the door on that strangely foggy December night. Then I had been determined to grade all of my senior papers before we broke for Christmas vacation and had stayed especially late to finish. Sal Vacarro, the school's maintenance man, had long ago entrusted me with a skeleton key for the academic building. Essentially, each teacher had their classroom key but a select few had the single key that unlocked all the other doors of the building, including the exit doors. A strange system, devised by the monks and never altered, but being one of the teacher's with the special key, I often graded in my classroom, so as not to fall lure to the myriad things at home I would rather be doing.

It was so strange to be in this hallway again, to move past the portrait of a distinctly brow-beaten monk of two centuries past. After greeting him, I had to put my book bag down and brace one arm against the door to open it. My classroom door always stuck, no matter how many times Sal oiled its hinges. When I opened it, the calming scent of my lavender sashays filled my nostrils. I stood there, doing nothing but breathing, for a few moments. The walk up the stairs, with my bag, had been more difficult than I would have imagined.

Besides wanting to flitter about my classroom in a September nesting ritual, I also needed to collect myself before entering back into the motions of the work day. Moreland was a small enough town and St. Augustine's a tight knit enough community that I had been in communication with almost all the people I desired to be. I knew the retired woman who had taken over my classes for the semester of my disability. Enough about my injuries and progress was known, and no doubt gossiped about, that I did not foresee too many redundant questions.

Yet I was afraid I could not face this day and all the others to come. The accident had certainly done something to the internal rhythms of my body. I was able to walk for hours, but grew tired standing for too long.

Focus on my physical self had become an unalterable part of my day. My pills were scheduled, my mental list of adjectives ready for selection each day I stumbled from my bed. Was my leg tight, achy, swollen, or unstable? Were the pains dull, electric, or sharp? Which exercises would I perform at my tri-weekly physical therapy sessions? These matters had been my reality for eight months while school, frankly, had not. It grew to be peculiarly comforting.

There was also more. Since the accident, I was conscious of a pervasive fear that, like the sound of one's breathing, could sometimes be ignored. But the effort to push it back required concentration and vigilance. Would I still be effective in the classroom when I felt so much menace around me? Would I again have the energy and stamina for all the duties expected of me at St. Augustine's, when my recovery was still ongoing?

Would, I asked myself, while arranging a stack of pretty notepaper, be struck by another car leaving this campus? Would I be left in the darkness, on the side of the road, with nothing but the grace of God to save me?

Chapter 1

"What do you think of the color?" Joe Torres asked as he slipped into a chair in the row behind mine. I tried to mask how startled I had been by his sudden proximity. My notebook was out and ready for our first faculty meeting but I was so distracted these days I did not even hear him enter.

I rolled my eyes in response. Every summer Sister Paul determined that the Towers and the academic building needed some form of cosmetic work. She kept Sal, the maintenance man, running from paint store to hardware store, convinced that teacher productivity would increase if we were simply in the correct environment. I, like most of the faculty, took silent umbrage to Sister's implication that our collective productivity needed improving. As a prep school with an exorbitant tuition, the faculty and administrative staff were suitably bedecked with degrees and honors.

Still I admired Sister's unwavering conviction that this one issue in her world could be solved. And now that my knee required habitual elevation I had new reason to appreciate the plush sofas in the faculty room. Those mammoth examples of Sister Paul's red period made the room look like the antechamber of a bordello, but they boasted deep cushions that induced more prep period napping than actual, waking productivity.

The conference room was now a rather shocking shade of cerulean, shocking most in its similarity to last year's color; one so brightly blue that several teachers claimed it gave them migraines on sunny days.

"Good God," my chairperson, Mark, said as he stumbled into the room. "I feel like I am in a fish tank."

"Or a Tidy Bowl toilet," Joe countered.

Our group was thus three. Joe was the art teacher, accustomed by the practice of his early morning art club to arriving early. Mark was always early. He was also the type of person who sat in the front row at meetings, fanning his many bags and binders around him. As a member of his department I was well aware that these burdens were merely props meant to suggest work, where little was actually done. My friend Ginny, also of the English department, griped constantly about Mark and how much better a chairperson she would be. But Mark had been a teacher at St. Augustine's for longer than she had and that was how things worked here.

I had never minded Mark in the least. He maintained a childish delight in subverting Sister's authority in small ways. He also professed such a lazy man's confidence in my abilities that I operated with very little oversight, practically composing my own yearly evaluations.

After settling himself and his possessions accordingly in the front row, Mark turned to greet the other chair people, who had arrived en masse and were somewhat perturbed to not be the first ones there. I contented myself with the obligatory nods, happy that our school hierarchy precluded much fraternization at full meetings. One on one, I have had pleasant dealings with the History chair, Elizabeth Maccabe, but we would neither sit next to each other at a faculty meeting nor chat openly about our mutual interests.

"Here's another change for you," Joe whispered, once again startling me. I followed his eyes to the door, where entered one of the guidance counselors, Toni Anne Tancredi and a tall man I did not know. Toni Anne had been a semi-professional dancer in her youth—now hardly past—and still maintained a weekend job at a dancing school. It was in the midst of aiding an enthusiastic but clumsy first grader that Toni Anne had tripped and done something dastardly to the tendons of her left foot.

I had made her better acquaintance over the summer, as we were both on the three day a week schedule at Moreland Physical Rehabilitation, a small center run by the father of one of St. Augustine's students. Tim Boone was a pleasant man and subsequently almost all of my interactions with him, his staff, and other patients were also pleasant. But now it

6

seemed I was on the verge of gossiping about Toni Anne, which I did not want to do.

"Who is he?" I asked Joe, barely moving my lips, so no hint of my curiosity showed.

"Ken Telford, the new English teacher. Was hired at the end of last year."

"Ah," I said, sweeping my gaze over the room as a whole before settling on the new teacher. Actually, my gaze paused first on Toni Anne's high heeled boots, and then sought Telford. His manner and appearance seemed to suggest a calculated kind of irreverence, one which no doubt appealed to teenagers. His tie was cartoonish, his hair a bit too shaggy, and I had no doubt that the very latest piece of gadgetry, masquerading as a cell phone, rested in his pocket. But he was ignoring Mark's wave with as much vigor as Mark was waving and I felt myself take an instant dislike to him.

His chair seemed noticeably closer to Toni Anne's than it should and my dark, petty, little mind immediately wondered if Ken was the boyfriend she had spent much of the summer blathering on about. Try as I might, I could not bring up any specific details of her gushing.

"He is from some prep school in the city. Just loves himself, doesn't he?" Joe asked disdainfully. As the resident cool teacher, I wondered if Joe's feelings were masking some jealousy. Admittedly I had also not taken well to the sight of this new man. Making a personal vow to reserve judgment at least until I had met him, I smiled silently. There were only four of us in the department and I was going to have to get along with Ken Telford.

"And," Joe said, before settling back in his own chair. "He's married."

Before I could form a reply to that, which should have been a non-sequitur but was not, the conference doors opened and the rest of the faculty streamed in. As if by some acknowledged but imaginary bell, they entered, with a moment to settle before Sr. Paul's procession. I smiled at Ginny, who had frantically moved her enormous bag out of the aisle, mere seconds before Sister swept by. Ginny always sat in an aisle seat at meetings.

She said she needed to race to the bathroom, at the conclusion of each one, to wash the veneer of hypocrisy from her skin.

I turned back to watch the administration enter. Sister led, naturally, and was followed by our vice Principal, Dolores Donovan. Whereas Sister only ever wore the somber habit of her order, Dolores possessed an apparently endless supply of coordinated outfits. I had yet to catch her obviously repeating herself and marveled at how it was possible to own that many pieces of clothing. Ginny and I had once driven past her normal sized home and concluded that the dining room and the third bedroom had to be reserved entirely for her multitudinous suits and matching shoes.

Behind Dolores was Jeremy Wrobleski, the Campus minister, Linda Mullen, the Dean of Students, and finally, the Athletic Director, whose pronounced limp and smaller stature made him seem a court jester to the decidedly more regal group ahead of him. Nick Morrison rarely spoke at these meetings, and once he entered, usually sat with the members of his coaching staff also on the faculty.

As was customary, we stood for prayer as soon as Sister Paul gave the nod. Jeremy was sincerely enamored of his own voice and tended to allow his prayers more style than substance. I felt my time better served with inattention and immediately began to fidget, switching from balancing on one leg to the other.

The slight curvature to the assembled rows allowed me to see Sal Vacarro at the end of the last one. Sal did not always guard his opinions as he should, and I could easily view the disgust etched in his face. Jeremy Wrobleski was an acquired taste and Sal clearly was not working very hard to like him. Besides his tendency towards verbosity, Jeremy was self serving and decidedly judgmental. A Polonius for this era, he also fancied himself an expert on almost everything and was never afraid to deliver a lecture on the very subjects you knew best in the world. I made it a practice to avoid him whenever possible.

Glancing past Sal, I once again caught the new English teacher, Ken, whispering in Toni Anne's ear. What was wrong with them? I was forced to pinch myself as a physical reminder that I was supposed to be reserving judgment. I hoped it wasn't judgmental to enjoy the way I saw Sister Paul's eyes narrow when they fell upon the couple.

"Thank you, Jeremy," she said, in a tone of finality and dare I say it, just a hint of weariness. Sr. Paul's fondness for Jeremy was never as high in his presence as it was wont to be when she spoke of him at a distance.

"We are gathered together today to inaugurate the ninety seventh year in the history of St. Augustine's." Sister paused, all but demanding our polite applause.

"There has been many exciting changes, some of which you can see," she said, lifting her arm to indicate the bright color around her. Here we were expected to turn our heads to look at the walls, attempting to convey a false surprise, as though we were seeing the garishness for the first time and marveling at Sister Paul's expert taste. Many of us were only able to accomplish this acting feat through years of steady practice.

"To begin, we welcome back Ms. Addra Lake, who has returned from her grievous injuries of last year."

I had expected some sort of announcement, though I considered it superfluous and completely mortifying. Seeing me, with the fading scars across my cheek and the cane at my side, seemed enough to announce both my return and the grievousness of my injuries. How stiffly I stood, to receive my own share of clapping, provided more evidence.

After returning to my seat, face scarlet and heart pounding, I was unable to follow the course of Sister's continued speech, and missed quite a bit.

"...Ken plans to help the revived school newspaper and helm the media arts club."

My head rose at hearing this, the knowledge that I would not be moderating the newspaper pierced through any remaining embarrassment. I also knew, without glancing his way, that Mark was providing the most vigorous applause.

He and I had spent the last few years dodging both student and administrative requests to revive the corpse of Ginny's school newspaper. She had left, harried and irritable, to go plan the Literary Arts Magazine. A bi-annual publication of delightfully misunderstood poets clearly bested the weekly newspaper, which was every year staffed by overeager investigative journalists.

If Ken wanted to ingratiate himself with the administration by taking on the student body's most verbose and sanctimonious members he most certainly could. A moment later, I delivered another pinch to my arm, having managed to be doubly judgmental with that last observation. Unfortunately both my criticisms and subsequent flagellation caused me to miss most of Sister's next announcement.

"Noah comes from a fine public school in Boston."

Noah, like myself and Ken before him, had to perform the half stand, half wave, that in a room crowded with chairs, inevitably meant you jostled someone next to you and spilled their coffee. His discomfit at doing this was endearing.

After Noah sat, Ginny caught my eye for a subtle roll of her own. We both knew that Sister Paul did not believe any fine public schools existed, despite much evidence to the contrary. She also refused to believe any could exist in an urban center.

I had not caught Noah's subject, or his last name for that matter, but judging from where he was seated, he must be the newest member of the science department. Perennially requiring new members, yet still remaining the only all-male department, the 'men of science,' as Ginny called them, were an interesting lot. They always sat together, in the last row of the conference room, and whispered presumably hilarious things to each other throughout the meetings. Save for those periods they came down in twos to commandeer the faculty copy machine, they preferred to take their prep periods in the small room in between the science labs, and mixed rarely with the rest of us.

I had had only vague dealings with the newest members of the department, regarding them as someone interchangeable. Not so with their oldest member, Stan Grimm. Suitably named, in my opinion, I had suffered through a prom committee chairpersonship with him. While I did all of the work, he monopolized the need to complain, insisting that Dolores Donovan had given him this duty as a punishment.

I was never able to determine what he had done to merit this punishment, nor form any but the worst opinion of his work ethic. At every occasion where his input was necessary he simply stared at me for a few moments before saying, "that's an interesting question." He would then walk away, without ever once attempting an answer.

Against my will I had found him fascinating. This decidedly contemptuous and unhelpful attitude with adults never seeped into his teaching. In fact the most deficient students raved about his ability to shape the complex universe into manageable, quantifiable dimensions. I had often desired to sit in on his organic chemistry class, were such collegiate activities allowed at St. Augustine's.

"…and Mr. Stabler and Ms. Lake will be a fine fit. Next, before Ms. Mullen updates all of you on the changes we have made to the student handbook, I would like to remind you that the Fall Festival and Fundraiser is only two weeks away. I will be putting committee sign-up sheets in your mailboxes by the conclusion of the day tomorrow."

The vice principal sat, seamlessly crossing her legs and taking a sip of her coffee. I looked at her, hoping to mask my consternation with a thoroughly sanguine expression. I needed to stop drifting away on my own thoughts. I had missed the transition from Sister Paul's opening, to the more 'nuts and bolts' pronouncements of our Vice Principal.

11

I also had no idea what I was well fitted to nor did I know to whom. Had Dolores said Mr. Smith? Mr. Stuben? Dolores Donovan's managerial genius half lay in your inability to hear her. In any given conversation, you were destined to miss at least forty percent as you strained to her measured whisper. Some teachers believed this tic to be one borne of nervous insecurity but I knew better. An overnight trip with the girls' soccer team acquainted me with just how loudly Dolores could project when properly motivated. The other faculty, having thus far no compulsion to stuff a toilet with tampons, knew nothing of her vocal wrath.

The whispering was a tactic, pure and simple. Dolores had long been tasked with seeing the plans of the principal put into actual practice. It was she who created the teacher schedules, organized the committees and meetings, and handled the secretarial staff. She managed this by foisting as much of it as possible on members of the faculty, whom it should be noted, were rarely compensated for doing a large share of her work, on top of their own.

My elation at avoiding newspaper duties was clearly a momentary reprieve. Dolores had me in her sights for something, and I tried not to snatch my "Welcome Packet" from Joe as he handed it over. The "Welcome Packet" was simply the embossed folder that contained what information teachers needed to start the year.

The Dean of Students, Susan Mullen, was talking about detention slips, tardy passes, and the annual changes to the Student handbook, while most teachers feigned attention. Our true attention was on the right hand side of our folder, which contained our schedule, duty roster, and class lists.

Knowing how little care the faculty would have for anything but the papers on the right side of the folder, Dolores had taken to instructing her secretary to copy them in colors garish enough to rival any Sister Paul chose for the walls. That way, the recalcitrant teachers could be summarily branded with the colors of the inattentive.

I had been studying the cheating methods of teenagers for a long time and took those lessons to heart. With an expert sleight of hand, my neon pink duty roster was encased in the pages of the massive student handbook. I could easily mimic interest in one while desperately searching the other.

"Please don't be yearbook. Please don't be yearbook."

My plea was valid and apparently not silent, as Joe offered me a sideways grin. He too must remember Donna Alvarez, the seemingly stalwart History teacher who walked out one chilly March morning. As yearbook moderator, she had been driven to the absolute edge by the students' inability to shape themselves into numbers for their graduation year photos. Felled by the complex lines and curves of the zero and the four, Donna had left the profession entirely. I knew I did not have the mental fortitude for yearbook duties.

But did I have the fortitude for the Honors Committee? I could not say, having no idea what it was. According to the note attached to the bottom of my roster, I was to have a meeting with Dolores and a Mr. Stabler at two o'clock to begin our planning. That gave me three hours, during which I would be at a Department meeting, to determine what the Honors Committee was, find this Mr. Stabler to see if he knew, and go to Dolores' office in the Towers with some kind of plan. Dolores always expected you to have a plan.

Feeing like I had avoided the firing squad only to be told my hanging was at two, I rose with the other teachers. The meeting was over and I had not heard anything the Dean of Students had said.

I turned a questioning glance towards Joe, who was already pursing his lips in well honed mimicry of Dean Mullen.

"Tardy students must receive detention. The fate of the universe rests upon those slips."

Laughing, Ginny stumbled over the row of chairs towards us. Her book bag had returned to its position in the aisle, forcing everyone to step over it in their quest for the door.

"Mark wants the department meeting in my room. Five Minutes."

She sighed eloquently, adjusting her cat's eyes glasses. Of course Ginny believed Mark chose this location for some Machiavellian purpose but she gave him too much credit. Her new room was spacious and situated closest to the side door that opened onto the parking lot path. Mark believed in quick exits, doors usually smacking behind him as dismissal was still being announced.

"Come on," Ginny said, grabbing my bag. "I want to make sure he isn't touching my stuff."

With a coordination that made me suspect prior planning, Joe took up Ginny's bag just as swiftly as she had taken mine. We exited the Towers, by design not speaking again until we were safely in the sun.

"It's stiff because I was sitting," I offered in explanation to no actual question.

"I will be able to walk faster in a minute."

"No worries, Addra." Joe said with a lazy smile. He was a good guy, with a lucky wife.

"I am my own department and have already adjourned my meeting."

As the only art teacher, Joe happily operated on the periphery of school life. Many of the job hassles, like department meetings, paper grading, and heavy book bags did not apply to him. Still, I reminded myself, he monitored teenagers while they handled scissors, turpentine, and paints that stained. I got vaguely nauseous simply visiting Joe in the art room.

"You want to come to ours?" Ginny asked. "We are planning lengthy lists of books for no one to read."

"*Macbeth* or *Hamlet*?" I asked.

"Dickens or Bronte?"

"*The Great Gatsby* or *Catcher in the Rye*?"

I grabbed Joe's arm in mock alarm.

"Girls hate *The Lord of Flies*, what can we do?"

Ginny grabbed his other arm and all but shrieked, "And boys won't read any poetry so we should never assign it!"

"Do tastes really fall in such strict gender lines?" Joe asked after prying us loose.

"No," Ginny said, shaking her graying curls.

"It isn't true all of the time, but it is expected to be true much of the time. You know how most teenagers are, they are so desperate to be in the 'normal' category that they will adopt attitudes they don't actually have."

Ginny had done her graduate work on gender based interpretations of literary texts, and had given the matter much thought.

"We do them a disservice by catering to any one group's supposed predilections."

"Yes," I agreed. "So we assign them *Beowulf* to make everyone equally unhappy."

I was actually proud that St. Augustine's English curriculum still exposed the students to much of the traditional literary canon. There were very good reasons these works had informed centuries of minds.

Of course I was not so deluded as to think the students were going to offer me thanks before sitting to take their summer reading exams tomorrow. We customarily assigned four books to be read from an approved list. Students were required to make journal entries about their reading as well as sit for an admittedly rigorous exam. The exam was so exacting in fact that it had become a half day affair that took place on the first day of school, with a general school orientation in the morning.

"Maybe you and Noah could work on that." Joe pointed out as we neared the side entrance to the academic building. I worried that I had lost the thread of the conversation again because that sounded decidedly like a non sequitur.

"Excuse me?"

Ginny laughed. "You really were out of it. Dolores chose you and the new man of science to revamp the Honors Program."

"Actually," Joe corrected, "I believe you are charged with aligning our program with current pedagogical trends."

I groaned. That was exactly the sort of thing Dolores would say. She spent part of her summer's catching up on her periodical reading, and always returned in the fall with some pet project meant to prove St. Augustine's educational merit.

"Do you think Noah...Stabler would know anything about current pedagogical trends in Honors Programs because I sure don't?"

Ginny whispered, "Honey, nobody does."

The whispering was necessary as we entered the building. Similar to the Towers, all due caution was necessary while walking the halls of the academic building at the start of the new school year. There were a myriad of projects to tackle and several of the faculty and the administration were always on the lookout for able bodied brethren to aid in the tackling.

You had to look askance at the person who only wanted a moment of your time or had a quick question. These were signs that you were about to be tricked into taking on tasks it was neither your responsibility nor interest to do. Looking down at my cane, I knew that I was the weakest of the herd and needed to be even more vigilant. I had been burned many times before, when well.

We entered Ginny's bright classroom, bidding Joe goodbye as we did. He waited until he had crossed back over the threshold, into the hall, before pointing to Ginny in silent but mirthful fashion. She certainly was a wrathful vision, flummoxed only by whom to yell at first: Mark, who was reading a magazine at her desk, or Ken, who was running a hand along the books in her case.

"We thought we would wait for you to begin," Mark said as he calmly slid his magazine into a manila folder and rose from his chair. Since meetings seemed easier to manage in classrooms rather than in Mark's cramped office in the Towers, we always took a few student desks and arranged a circle to sit in. Generally we each left a desk to our left for books and papers. Since Ken still had his back turned, we made the circle without him.

"Tests?" Mark said at the same time Ginny and I were already opening our bags to retrieve the folders.

It was the practice at St. Augustine's for teachers to give their departmental exams to their chairperson for review. If no mistakes were found, the chairperson gave the tests to the secretarial staff to copy. At no time was a mere teacher to hand over an exam to the office. We knew that Mark did little more than flip through our exams to note the page count before submitting them. By mutual agreement then, he did not question any of our test questions and we did our best to submit exams sans mistakes.

As I watched out of the corner of my eye, Ken continued to peruse Ginny's book selections. He seemed not at all inclined to join the meeting though, pinching myself, I recalled that as a new teacher Ken would be administering tests we had created anyhow.

In a school the size of St. Augustine's it was impossible to avoid students having the same teacher more than once. To ensure that the punishment of this was not too severe for either teacher or student, typically our four person department divided into pairs. One pair took on the bumbling ninth graders and the juniors, while the other taught sophomores and the seniors. Allowing that year grace period permitted all concerned to recover from their dealings with the others. It was currently my job to teach the sophomores and the seniors, as it seemed, was Ken's.

Since this division flip-flopped every few years, each of us read through the approved reading lists of the others. The textbook was generally augmented by two to three other tomes. We hashed out what needed to be hashed out until we reached a consensus for what each teacher would be assigning during the year.

It took thus a mere matter of moments to pass through each other's suggestions, with a nod here and a grimace there. Every one of us had our favorites, Mark generally preferred the things he had taught the longest, Ginny loved plays. I preferred poetry, if for no other reason, than a poorly received example could be dismissed in a class period, as opposed to a lengthy novel that the students would be forced to hate for months. Still, the time had come again for *Hamlet* and *Jane Eyre* so I was doubly contented.

Ken continued to do nothing, increasing not only my ire, but the number of red marks dotting my arms. Clearly my attempts to stop judging him were failures. I dared not even look at Ginny knowing full well that it would soon be she, and not Mark, who would have to bid Ken to contribute something to this meeting.

Within a few seconds, perhaps sensing these feelings, Ken turned around to face us. After seeing the way our desks were arranged, he strode to the front of the room, and sat casually upon the top of Ginny's desk, extending his long legs to rest upon a chair in front of him.

"We need to shake things up a bit, don't we? These same books are assigned every year in every school."

No one answered him for a moment; I intended to do nothing but pinch myself until he stopped talking.

"What do you suggest?" Mark asked, doing a fine job keeping his voice neutral.

"Why not make a cut off year and say we will assign nothing that was written before 1960? Or anything written by a European? We need to throw off these tropes and these rules."

Noticing that no one was actually answering him, he proceeded to rattle off increasingly impossible books for the students to read. It wasn't that his suggestions were necessarily inappropriate, and certainly not for college students or high school seniors in a college preparatory program. But they were so for the culture of St. Augustine's. I briefly wondered how astute Ken could be if he missed the most obvious characteristic of this school's character.

"How about the seniors don't read any published works at all? Have the course be purely self actualizing?"

"Self actualizing?"

"What school did you teach at before here?"

Mark had asked the former question and Ginny the latter, since she had less care for how her direct questions might be received.

Naturally, Ken chose to answer Mark, as I imagine anyone would.

"The students would only read and critique works that their classmates had written. Combine a creative writing curriculum with one that allows them to experience the sharing of their souls outpouring with others."

I am by nature a quiet person, so I certainly had no answer to that, but an image of Ken in college did come unbidden to my mind. I had no trouble picturing the silly, earnest girl who would fall for his nonsense, nor the distinctly herbal odor that no doubt draped his dorm room.

'Look, Ken" Mark began. "Our curriculum always allows for some yearly adjustments, but the parents here want their children prepared for competitive colleges. That means designing our courses in rough approximation to other prestigious high schools."

I looked out the window, where I only saw the pathway to the parking lot, but could picture the stone façade of the Towers. Both that building and this one had stood erect against one hundred and fifty years of change, and, in the last century, teenagers. It could easily weather the tempest of Ken Telford's adolescent attempts at non-conformity.

"What about the newspaper then?" He asked, managing to only sound slightly belligerent.

"What about it?" Mark countered, genuinely perplexed.

"Do you all help me with it?"

That question naturally earned him an outright laugh from Mark while Ginny only shook her head. I merely pinched myself again, this time to stop the flow of giggles that threatened to erupt. Was it possible Ken's entire resume had been a 'self actualizing' bit of fiction? How did he not know how a school worked?

"Ken, newspaper is an extracurricular club. You receive a stipend for moderating it. It has nothing to do with the English department."

Mark said this with conviction. No one would manipulate him into doing extra work. He based his entire career on that unwavering belief. I might have had a bit of sympathy for Ken, if he legitimately had not realized what an awesome task was before him. But then I recalled that re-vamping the Honors Program came with no stipend.

"The student editors have everything set up already." Ginny answered him.

"The copy is plugged into a computer program that does the layouts and each edition is emailed to the company that prints it. Your job is really to do the final edits and approve the content."

She thought for a moment and then continued.

"Just remember where you are and that parents, alumni, and sponsors also receive copies."

"What does that mean?"

"No editorials supporting drugs, sex, and rock and roll." Mark said.

"No criticisms of the tuition, the uniforms, or the price of food in the cafeteria," Ginny added while I was left wondering what else the students would even wish to talk about. Those complaints were on the hit parade of all high-schoolers, though every generation of teenagers believed themselves the inventors of the squeaky wheel.

"Can I get a co-moderator?" Ken asked. "Someone from a different department?"

"I don't see why not." I responded, realizing this was the first thing that I had said directly to him.

"Whom do you have in mind?" I asked sweetly, though I already knew the answer. I wondered how much interest Toni Anne had in journalism or if that even mattered.

"If that is all…" Mark stated more than asked as he reached into his bag.

Ginny and I also pulled out our Welcome Packets, for the time had come to finally look over our class lists. We would learn which of our favorite and least favorite students were back in our classes. When we teachers gathered together in groups it was possible to drop the façade that we were equally content to teach any and all students.

"Damn," Ginny muttered. "I have Donnelly again."

"Which one, Kyle or Maggie?" I asked.

"Doesn't matter, their father always tries to record our conversations."

I giggled. "Amanda Cardelli's mom brought a calculator to the report card meetings, so she could check my math."

"I have Seth Meyers," Mark noted. "Isn't he a problem?"

I shook my head.

"Some teachers always say that about him but he isn't at all. Seth is brilliant. He won't take any notes and he will always keep his head down. But he will be your answer key for every test you give."

Ginny sighed. "I seem to have every varsity football player in the eleventh grade in my third period class. How did that happen?"

I also had an answer for her.

"That is going to happen now that Coach Brown is on staff. He will be running a special gym period for the players. The rest of their schedules have to align because of it."

"He can do that?" Ken asked, his tone indicating that he had no problem with snap judgments of his colleagues.

"I would not say Coach did it exactly. He and the Athletic Director, Nick Morrison, probably came up with the idea and Nick brought it to Dolores and Sister Paul."

Ken shook his head. "Every school is the same."

I just looked at him for a long moment, knowing at one time or another, every person in this room had whispered about some special treatment a member of a sports team had received or some money that went to the athletic department over the academic ones.

However, to be fair, the most competitive private schools also offered competitive sports programs, and our football team had long been our most successful. I could well imagine the amount of revenue our home games generated. In fact, I did not have to imagine it. Our new, professional looking sports facilities had been built on the strength of that revenue as well as the significant contributions of sport playing alumni.

"How do you know this?" Ginny asked, referring back to the issue of the special gym class. She was justifiably incredulous. Details about the running of the athletic department had always been shrouded in mystery. Indeed, Sister Paul had apparently not even announced that Coach Brown was now a member of the faculty.

"P.T." I answered, prompting Ken to ask what that was.

"Physical Therapy. I go to a facility run by Tim Boone, the father of one of our seniors."

I quickly checked my lists. Laurie Boone was in my class. I had made her better acquaintance over the summer as well, when she did some filing for her father.

"There is only one therapy place in Moreland, otherwise you need to drive up to Binghamton. A lot of the boys on the team go for treatment or physical evaluations there. They talk."

I briefly toyed with the idea of telling Ken that Toni Anne also talked and talked while she was at physical therapy but decided against it. Perhaps they were barely knew each other. There were some men and women who always appeared to flirt with whomever they were near.

"I even saw Coach Brown there a few times. He offered to arrange for his boys to help me manage around campus and back and forth to my car."

I meant to say this in a matter of fact way, but heard my voice catch anyway. I barely knew the coach but he had made arrangements to aid me in a way designed to make me feel less embarrassed for not having to ask for help. I knew most of the football team, they were happy for any chance to lift heavy objects so I did not have to feel self conscious in front of them.

Indeed, after running into a few of them at therapy, in my sweat pants and silly tee shirts, I stopped caring about how I looked. In my experience even the surliest student within school delights in seeing their teachers out of it.

"Maybe having Coach around will be a good thing. Sister is definitely worried about money this year, and the sports program is our quickest route to more of it."

As a chairperson, Mark attended more meetings with Sister and was occasionally privy to fiduciary information that was deemed above the clearance level of us lowly teachers. Without a doubt, Sister ran her school like a secretive, government operation.

"All private schools have money troubles," Ken said dismissively.

I wondered how true that was. St. Augustine's did give some academic scholarships but we were generally a school for the well to do and our tuition made that fact quite clear. Why would Sister Paul be worried about money?

Well," Mark began, standing. "There are sandwiches in the cafeteria. Why don't you head down? I have to go drop these tests off to Bernadette. We can get out of here at two."

He delivered his last comment with a sympathetic glance in my direction.

"Heard about your meeting. Sorry."

Checking that his magazine folder and his test folder were separated in his bag, Mark gathered up his things and left. Ken followed, giving us a vague stare that I decided to take as a friendly farewell.

"That one is going to be a problem." Ginny said in his wake. I agreed with her, not even bothering to pinch myself again.

"I'll take your bag. Mine can stay here."

I watched her lock up the room, checking both doors, since she had two. I managed to exit with only one catch of my cane under a desk, an impressive feat for me.

"Come on. We are going to celebrate our labors with a slowly eaten sandwich. You can't do anything about your honors meeting until you find out what Dolores' angle is."

Ginny was right. Dolores generally had at least one ulterior motive behind every seemingly innocuous plan she made. I could only claim to have figured out half of them in time to avoid extraneous work.

Not having any expectation of seeing Noah Stabler at lunch, I figured that the other men of science could explain to him that a two o'clock meeting with Dolores always began at 1:50.

"Dolores, how are you? I love that color."

Having settled myself with some difficulty into one of the two plush chairs facing her desk, I thought I should be try to deflect any comment on my own slightly defeated appearance.

"Why thank you, Addra. How are you holding up?"

"Oh, fine, fine."

I looked around her office, to find something worthy of initiating a topic change. I supposed I could compliment Dolores' shoes, which were the same burnished color as her suit. Of course the shoes were leather, while the suit was most likely silk. I refused to look down at my own clothes.

"Coach Brown says the boys will begin helping you out tomorrow?"

"Yes," I said, somewhat surprised. "It is wonderful of the coach to do this."

"It is, but you do deserve it. Those boys have a fine sense of chivalry too."

I was not entirely sure how true that was, given what I had seen of teenaged romances. But I was more curious to know how Dolores had come by the knowledge of the coach's arrangement. I tried to picture her on the football field, her delicate heels sinking into the dirt, but could not.

'Noah, I hope nothing serious kept you?"

Having already taken my seat, I did not wish to turn around and gape at the newly arrived Mr. Stabler. But I did hear the slight hesitation in his step as he both entered and absorbed the meaning behind Dolores' words.

How could he answer her? If no calamity had befallen him he would be admitting to simply arriving late, a transgression he no doubt realized was serious to Dolores. His eyes were on her desk clock, which read 2:02. Still staring at it, he tripped over my cane and more or less fell into a chair.

"It takes a while to navigate these halls. I still take a wrong turn now and again." I was speaking more to Dolores than him, but I felt I owed him, since I had put my cane down without thinking of his arrival.

"Noah Stabler. It is nice to meet you Addra."

"You as well, Noah. I trust you had time for lunch?" I raised my eyebrows slightly.

"No, net yet. We were unpacking some things in the chemistry lab and taking inventory."

"Excellent," Dolores breathed. Now that the meeting was about to begin she lowered her voice. I pitched forward in my seat to increase my chances of hearing her.

"We won't be long here, and I am sure the cafeteria will have something for you when we are finished."

She looked down at the papers on her desk, which allowed Noah time to glance in my direction. Had I been an entirely different sort of person I would have winked.

"I chose you for this committee, Addra, because you have taught honors classes for so long. Noah, being new, will bring a fresh perspective."

She stopped here to look at us, as if expecting some response. This time neither Noah nor I looked at each other. Taking up the mantle of seniority, I said, "ah."

"We are just in fact gathering mode at this point." She paused again.

"Fact gathering." Noah repeated.

"Precisely. How are the honors courses actually different from the general classes? How do the grades break down and distribute in comparison? Are we able to say that the Honors students score the highest on standardized tests? Do they receive the most scholarship money to good schools? These are the facts we need."

She slid a frighteningly thick folder towards me. I presumed all of the facts were contained within it, since only the administration and their secretaries had access to such things. And now I and the newest man of science did as well. The only question that remained was why.

"So we will meet again next week, and see where we are."

Dolores stood, indicating that we were to do so as well. I was flummoxed, though maybe Noah had no way to realize that something was amiss. We were being dismissed with no list of difficult tasks to perform in an absurdly short period of time. No further meeting had been definitively scheduled. I always left Dolores confused, but generally my confusion was borne over how much work she managed to have me agree to do. I usually thanked her for my burden as well. Now I walked with precious little to actually do. If I understood her, I was look over some figures and Noah would make an impressive looking spread sheet that took the same figures and arranged them in another way.

I gathered my cane and turned to say goodbye, noting that Noah had already picked up my book bag.

"I apologize for giving you both such unglamorous work. You could hardly talk about it without boring people."

"Ah, yes." I said, trying to back out of the room, though my leg usually protested such motion. When I had just cleared the threshold, Dolores shut the door.

I followed Noah down the staircase and out the front door of the Towers. We did not speak, nor did we encounter anyone, though surely at least Sister Paul remained.

"So what was that?" Noah asked as he sat down on one of the stone benches that lined the garden outside the Towers.

"I have no idea, but trust me, it was peculiar." I paused for a moment before continuing.

"And we are not supposed to talk about it with anyone."

"Ah," he said, a smile in his voice.

I turned towards him to laugh, enjoying his quick study of my habits.

"You can borrow that, but you can't steal it. 'Ah' has allowed me to talk for over ten years without actually saying anything."

"Is that how it is here?" He took off his glasses to wipe them, though they seemed perfectly clear to me. I avoided looking at him when I answered.

"I think it is like that everywhere. You have to carefully choose your friends, assume you have enemies, and keep your head down when you feel a disturbance in the air."

"Like war?"

Looking down at the causality of my leg, I said, "sometimes."

"You have worked in schools before, you know how it is."

"I do, but it is different here. Up in the science wing I feel like I am in a frat house. In the Towers…"

"An English drawing room comedy?"

Noah laughed again, a sound I liked.

"Yes but I am not sure it is funny in the ways it should be."

The sun was getting lower in the sky largely obscured by the trees that dotted the campus. I could hear the sounds of the football practice and felt a cool breeze on my arms. I was comfortable for the first time all day.

"Should we plan something on our own to tackle this Honors business?" Noah asked.

I thought for a moment. I would have a few hours free tomorrow, since Summer Reading Exams were being given at noon and 1:30, and I was only obliged to attend the opening student orientation and homeroom.

"What grade do you have for your homeroom?"

"I don't have a homeroom, something about a lab prep period in the morning."

"Lucky man," I grinned, though I did not exactly mean it. Were it not for the announcements in homeroom, and the occasional gleaned tidbit from the students, I would never know what was going on.

"So I will be free between 10:30 and 11:45, before the summer reading tests. We could meet in my classroom. I'm in 2G."

"Great. Let me walk you to your car. Do you have someone to help you get these books in the house?"

"No worries there, since I don't intend to take them out of the trunk. The only way to prepare for the summer reading exams is to vegetate in front of the television, bowl of ice cream in hand."

"That bad?"

"It is when you recall that the student journals were your idea, in addition to the test with three essays."

We reached my car, a Volkswagen Beetle that I was quite fond of, despite the leg pain that accompanied driving it.

Belatedly I wondered if Noah had asked about getting my books inside because he was curious about my living situation. Brushing my hair away from the scar on my cheek, I also wondered if I was more concerned about reminding him it was there or myself.

28

"Is that yours?"

The only other car in the lot was an ancient station wagon.

"Sadly, yes. Could I possibly convince you that it is yours?" He took my keys from my hand, unlocked my trunk, and hefted the books inside.

"Maybe, I have been pretty distracted lately. Like a kid, I look forward to the first day of school, but dread it at the same time."

"How are the kids here, by the way? No one even mentioned them today."

"The kids are great; they are the best part of every day. That will be important to remember." I lifted my hand to beckon for my keys.

"It was really nice to meet you Noah."

"You too, Addra."

I wanted to say something else but could think of nothing. I no longer felt comfortable, but was instead feeling a thousand other things. I carefully got into my car, took a few deep breathes, and drove away. Every time I checked, Noah was still watching me.

Chapter 2

The morning did not come soon enough nor did it come easily. Once I was awake and drinking my coffee, the oppressiveness of my nightmares began to fade. It hurt though, like the moment of going from blissful warmth to bracing chill.

I no longer spent time trying to recall the exact nature of my dreams. The impressions I awoke with were enough; the smell of leaves, the sound of my rain coat rustling underneath me. Being left broken on the side of that road was the worst part of my ordeal. There was no recovery from something you could not forget.

Perhaps that is why, when taking my required walk, I usually went back to the street where the accident occurred. It was a cul de sac, and walking to it also meant walking around it and back out onto the same street. I had known most of the homeowners on 10th Street by sight but now routinely chatted with many of them, seeing them so often.

I also considered it a good will gesture for the school. The 10th Street cul de sac abutted the ending of the alley that ran behind the athletic fields. Though the football field had been placed as far into the campus as possible, with the relatively quiet track laid out closest to the alley, there was still quite a bit of residual noise in the neighborhood.

In the beginning, when my walking had been most slow and ponderous, I would walk from home, go through the alley, and use the school's track. It now felt like defeat to do so.

I enjoyed my walks more now, especially since autumn had finally been called forth from behind a rather humid summer. It was embarrassing to admit how many years I had spent continuing to drive to school, while living in a small house eight blocks away. I comforted myself in the knowledge that I would emerge from my recovery, ironically, in the best shape of my life.

This was the first day of school for the students, and they were being allowed a later arrival time of 8:30 to begin their orientation. Beginning tomorrow, I would be required at work by 8:00, but in truth, I arrived much earlier as part of a small group of faculty and administration who did the same.

Desiring that very thing today, I tried to make my walk as brisk as possible, but needed to stop when I saw Mitch and Wanda Doyle out on their stoop. I was not surprised to see the retired couple. Unrepentant smokers, by mutual agreement they would not smoke indoors and could be found on their front steps at all hours.

"Good morning, Addra. Are you ready for the big day?"

I stretched a bit, having stopped to greet them.

"Wanda, I am not even sure. How about you guys? The kids with the new cars are going to be up this block again."

Students were not allowed to park on campus, though the idea was broached yearly. Many of them, taking advantage of the alley, parked along 10th. Mitch and Wanda took the invasion with greater grace than many in the cul de sac, possibly because they had a wide driveway and garage.

"We have enjoyed the quiet, I won't lie. And I will miss seeing you," Wanda answered.

"Yeah, kid, you gave us someone to talk to besides each other." Mitch lit a cigarette with the butt of the one he had just finished.

"No, I will still be walking in the mornings, when I can. It won't be for as long, but I am going to try not to take my car every day."

"Good, we like to set my watch by you and the old man, don't we Wanda?"

"Old man?"

"Yeah, some little, old guy, walks around here too. You haven't seen him? Pitiful thing. But he is out here a lot, and that is saying something. Like you!"

I wanted to think that Mitch meant my dedication to recovery 'said something,' and not that I was also a pitiful thing. Residual worry about resuming work was making me a bit negative this morning. I needed to get to school and distract myself with all the tasks of the day.

"Well guys, I am heading back for a quick change. I need to drive to work today for all the bins of tests and journals I will have by the end of it."

I had been boring them with my complaints about the dreaded summer reading exams since August. It was then that I usually began expounding on how much easier it would be if I taught math. Of course I still performed addition computations by wiggling each of my fingers in turn so this all mere speculation.

After bidding Mitch and Wanda goodbye, I completed my trek around the cul de sac, faintly catching Coach Brown's raised voice on the wind as I passed the alley. Mr. Delgado, who lived in the oldest home on the block had wires strewn about his lawn, and a ladder lying on its' side. I briefly wondered if he could be decorating for Halloween, in contrast to everything I had observed about the curmudgeon. But my thoughts soon turned inward. The screws lodged in my knee ached on damp mornings and I wanted to return to my bed, perhaps dreaming of Noah Stabler's smile, more than I wanted to face anything in my upcoming day.

"Hey Sal!" I called from the parking lot. The maintenance man was walking over from the football field, a bag of garbage in his hand. We reached the pathway to the academic building at the same time, a testimony to how stiff I was after the drive.

"Those boys are pigs Addra and the coach is no better. Every morning I fill a whole bag. Do they practice on that field or just eat?"

He was obviously not expecting an answer so I did not give one. Sal was probably not interested in my jealousy over the aforementioned eating habits of the growing teenage boy. During cafeteria duty it was hard not to simply stare as the football team pooled their collective lunches, each one of them bringing the equivalent of four normal sized meals from home. Once this take was augmented by the French fries, burgers, and bagels they purchased from the cafeteria, the boys could barely see each other over the mound. They all ate in silence until their brethren became visible on the other side.

I was only walking toward the building with my purse, intending to take a look at the Honors folder before I had to head down to the cafeteria for student orientation. I also liked to match the students in my homeroom to their desks and their materials had already been delivered to my room. Placing schedules and handbooks on each desk before their arrival allowed for a more smooth transition to the new school year. Nothing was worse than having twenty awkward kids, with heavy back backs extended behind them, crowding in a single doorway. I also considered having a 9th grade homeroom to be a special burden. Establishing good habits here would go a long way in acclimating them to the school.

After my classroom was arranged, I realized I still had well over an hour before the students were set to arrive. Ironically, given my intentions, I had left Dolores' folder in the trunk of my car. Grabbing my cane, I exited the building, and resolved not to be angry with anything that provided more exercise for my tight muscles. Still forgetting the very thing I had wanted to remember was frustrating.

My car was not the only one in the lot, nor had it been when I first arrived. Sister Joseph and Dolores Donavan had an ongoing competition to see which could arrive the earliest. The math chairperson, Scott Pearson, all but lived here, as did the Athletic Director, though I did not see his little sports car. So my eye was immediately drawn to the green, hatch-backed car I saw in the far corner of the lot. I wondered if a senior had arrived early and hoped no one would notice their new car residing in one of the back spots.

Checking for such things, which were not uncommon occurrences, was usually Sal's job, but seeing as I was already here, I kept glancing back at the car as I stood rummaging through my trunk.

Dolores' folder seemed even thicker this morning, and I wondered anew what her plans for this committee really were. She clearly held some suspicion, and was intending for Noah and I to provide outside corroboration of it. This manipulation angered me, since her job security was more assured than ours. Would she be hanging us out to dry?

My head was beginning to hurt and I was becoming increasingly suspicious of both Dolores and the car behind me. There it was again, the feeling of menace that lurked beneath every act of my day. Being a firm believer in the power of deep breathing, I stood for a few moments doing only that before slamming my trunk shut.

If I were really curious or worried about the presence of this unknown car I would approach it. Better still I would simply recognize that I had been gone from this place for eight months. How would I really know which cars belonged and which did not?

Taking up my cane, and clutching the folder in my other hand, I headed back up the path towards the academic building. But self disgust can be distracting much like cobblestones can be perilous to an inattentive woman with a cane. I did not go down but the folder did, scattering the papers in a lovely pattern on the lawn.

Unable to bend for long periods of time, I was forced to sit on a bench and maneuver my good leg and arms to reach each page one by one. Trying to convince myself that this too must count as exercise, I only realized my position obscured me from sight of the parking lot when I heard a car door slam.

Actually, I noted, my hand stilled in the act of picking up one damp page, I heard two doors slam. Grabbing my cane I moved with as much alacrity as I could muster toward the safety of a copse of trees, leaving some papers in my wake.

There was only a moment for me to feel foolish before I heard the tapping of Toni Anne Tancredi's heeled boots. She was staring straight ahead and seemed to notice neither me nor the papers littering the lawn. I only needed wait a few seconds more, since the Guidance department was housed on the first floor of the Towers, and Toni Anne would be out of view.

Of course nothing prevented me from stepping out from behind the trees and running directly into Ken Telford who was also coming from the parking lot. Neither one of us said anything, though I waved my messy handful of papers, expecting them to explain my presence on the lawn. He blinked once or twice and then walked on past me.

Sighing I resumed my recently vacated bench to finish gathering my file. Not knowing what to think, I only paused to wave at Sal, who was hiding behind a tree on the other side of the path.

"Hey Addra," Joe beckoned from his position on the far wall of the cafeteria.

The opening orientation for students always took place in the cafeteria instead of the auditorium. Sister Paul traded looking at the backs of half the students for the ability of all of them to use the table tops to complete their census forms and read through their handbooks.

"Why are you here? You don't have a homeroom."

"Mark is going to be a bit late," he said with a wink. "Car trouble."

"Ah," I answered, knowingly. I should have expected this.

Mark leased a new luxury model vehicle every two years. The chance of actual car trouble was low compared to the likelihood that he had mounted passive protest against yesterday's holiday meeting. Needless to say Joe also covered Mike's homeroom the day before Thanksgiving and on the day of Christmas mass and homeroom parties.

I waved at Ginny, holding up the wall opposite us. Between us, the students began to file in, naturally adhering to a seat order that marked them by age and position. The seniors were ensconced in the bank of tables furthest from the doors, along a row of windows.

As was customary, their cool status quelled most of their desire to make noise, leaving the most vocal posturing to the juniors beside them. I periodically waved to a few students, but this time was for fraternizing with each other. It was most important to greet people one had spent the summer seeing, as well as for new couples to present themselves to the group. I watched Laurie Boone walk in on the arm of the quarterback, Johnny Marchiano.

Before I could give that budding romance any thought, several small students caught my eye.

"I'll be back," I said to Joe, ignoring his head shake.

"Hi, there. Welcome to St. Augustine's," I said to a group of clearly ninth grade students. They stood frozen in the doorway of the cafeteria.

"The newest students usually sit right here," I said, indicating the row of long tables closest to the door. More than one in the group looked grateful to not have to walk any deeper into the room, which would take them past the boisterous older kids.

I ushered the first set over and then returned to the door to repeat the process. My heart cracked open, seeing how stiffly the freshmen moved in their uniforms. I could practically smell the pleasant, plastic scent of new notebooks and book bags.

"Why can't we have a separate freshmen orientation?" I whispered furiously to Ginny, who had walked over to help.

"Trial by fire," she answered back, not bothering to whisper.

It was true, for all the precepts of faith our school was meant to model, Sister Paul had a decidedly Darwinian approach to the training of new students and faculty.

Once we approached 8:30 and reached seating capacity, I left Ginny at the door and returned to Joe's perch. The administration would be entering in their

36

procession and I doubted it would have the same effect it had yesterday. In fact, little of the coming speeches would have much impact upon me, other than the effort it would take to stifle sighs and eye rolls. Perhaps it was dangerous to sit so close to Joe who had a tendency to feel the weight of school based irony more than I.

I motioned for a group of sophomore's to squeeze a bit more in their row, so that I could sit down. Dedicating myself to the reading of the Student Handbook, in preparation for the questions that would inevitably be asked in homeroom, I pledged to ignore any and all speaking that I heard around me. It seemed the safest course of action.

"Are you all right?" I heard concern in Noah's voice as he entered my classroom to find me at my desk, head in hands.

I quickly straightened, hoping the position had not done shocking things to my hair, but refusing to look as though I cared. My students had just been dismissed from their first homeroom.

"Fine. Freshmen." I said by way of explanation.

They had been adorable and utterly confused, as predicted. We went over the handbook twice, for good measure, and had a crash course on the reading of their schedules, which divided their days into letter based periods. This, on its own, should have produced no brow furrowing, considering the more than decade which had passed since they mastered their alphabets. However I was also forced to explain that their first class of each day was actually period B, since homeroom was delineated period A. There was also the matter of having different classes, at different times, depending on what day it was in the eight day cycle used by the school. Informing them that the cycle days were also delineated by letters had been met with groans.

"So I could have your class, in room 2G, during period B on day C but at period G on day E?" One sweet looking girl, Ella Arnez, had asked.

I almost hated to answer her.

"Yes, and also be mindful that certain periods, on certain days, meet for more mods than others."

"Ms. Lake, what is a mod?"

"It is shortened from the world module, it is a fifteen minute block of time. Notice, some classes on your schedule, like art, always meet for three mods or forty five minutes. But you could have a course, like religion, that only meets three days during the cycle, but meets for four or five mods at a time."

"Could you explain that again?" A tall boy, asked from the back, without raising his hand. That needed to be corrected before I went through the schedule madness again. They did not seem comforted by my claim that it would all make more sense after they stopped expecting it to make sense. This would be a trial by fire indeed, and most freshmen would arrive late to all their classes until October.

I had sent them, with a senior guide, to their religious service orientation, at 10:15. This would be followed by the summer reading exams, proctored by most members of the faculty, save for us in the English department. Ginny had already left cardboard boxes in each classroom, for students to deposit their reading journals into when they entered their testing room.

As English teachers, Ginny, Mark, and Ken would quietly go from room to room, once the exams had begun, and remove the boxes so we could begin organizing the journals for review. Coach Brown had arranged a senior football player to fetch my sophomore journals from the first exam seating, and then collect the others after his own exam was through.

I shook my head, alarmed that our logistical preparations might be more convoluted than necessary, and turned back to Noah.

"Sorry, seeing the school through the eyes of new, frightened students, is pretty draining."

"You should see it through my eyes too." He pulled over the full sized chair I kept near my desk, and placed a bag of granola in front of me.

"It isn't much, but we should not skip lunch for this."

"Thanks," I said. "So how is it all through your eyes, at least so far?"

I was genuinely curious to know, since I could still easily recall how overwhelming I had found the workings of this school when I first arrived. It could also be frustrating, for a teacher of experience, to be in a place whose practices rarely altered, no matter how salient a reason there might be for change.

"So far, I feel safest in the lab, where I have some control. But otherwise...I keep hearing the word protocol. It isn't exactly what I envisioned when I applied here."

"Protocol always makes me feel like we are in the military. It is definitely at odds with the beauty of this landscape and the romance of the buildings."

I paused here to chew some granola, wondering if it would be in poor taste to pull out my candy bar now. I also hoped Noah understood I referred to the pleasingly gothic buildings and tendency of the wind to draw music forth from the trees. I hardly meant that actual coupling was sought out here. Though given what I had stumbled upon this morning, I may well need to expand the connotation of the word.

I might also have to explain what had befallen the Honors file, when I placed it, bedraggled and still damp, on the table.

"There may have been an issue with clumsiness." I said. "And gravity."

He laughed and I wondered why he had left Boston to come here.

"Why don't we start by laying some of these on the desk and matching them to their counterparts? Looks like we have student transcripts and what? College admissions and scholarship data?"

"Yes, and remember the names on those will be for students who have already graduated. I am not sure what exactly Dolores wants, but I think it has something to do with the students in the current program."

"What makes you say that?"

"I am not sure. But I feel like we are pawns in some game so I don't want to devote too much energy to this until we discover just what is going on."

"I agree. Besides, Dolores mentioned determining if Honors classes are substantially different from non Honors ones, correct? We don't have the authority to request teacher exams or lesson plans, so right away, we can forget that one. All I can do is attest that my own classes will be run differently."

"Mine as well."

Once all the college information was put back in page order and clipped with one of my flower topped clips, we turned to the alphabetizing of the transcripts, which would be done after we separated them into grade level.

"So it looks like the majority of students enter the program as freshmen?"

"Yes, there is a program admission test that is given during the summer. Once, a few years ago, chairpeople were permitted to see it, but the test was designed and is always administered by Dolores and Sister."

"But you can enter the program at a later date?"

"Yes," I responded, not pausing in my alphabetizing of the senior transcripts, having taught them all before.

"It is arguably more difficult, because you have to have maintained a 97 average in your regular courses and have to complete the Honors level of community service and extra projects."

"Plus, and I hate to say this, because there is a lot of debate amongst the teachers on this score, but the Honors courses have weighted grade averages, since they are supposed to be more challenging."

Interrupting me, though pleasantly, Noah said, "so a student wanting to make the program later could claim that their high grades have more merit because they are not weighted?"

"But that is only providing that the Honors and non-Honors courses are taught too similarly, otherwise there really is no advantage. The argument festers because it is hard to prove. A lot of teachers like the Honors Program because,"

"Because they may run it with the thought that,"

"Smarter students,"

"Less work for them?" Noah popped some granola, managing a small sigh at the same time.

"Not only that, the Honors students have the prestige of a different diploma, class trips, symposium courses that meet at different locations. I am not sure that they or their parents are going to argue if the courses are not all as challenging as they could be."

"So…what? Do you know which side Dolores comes down on?"

"I never know what Dolores really thinks. I love the program, and most of the students in it are incredibly motivated. But there is a cap on the numbers, and you could argue, for instance, that there is a disproportionate number of athletes in the program."

Noah, had been alphabetizing again, looked up when I said that.

"Is Leonard Jamison an athlete?"

I thought for a moment. "Yes, Junior football player. Why?"

"Well, the Honors course delineations on his transcript do not start until his sophomore year, but he does not have anything near a 97 average in all his classes as a freshman. Is it average, or 97 in each class?"

"Average, though obviously you cannot be outrageously far from the mark in anything." I leaned to the side to look at what Noah was seeing.

"But Leonard has a 72 in religion and a 78 in math. Could his average still…"

Noah shook his head, and I presumed, with some envy, that he could do the calculation in his head.

"Maybe there is some kind of mistake," I said, "Why don't we go through the rest of them and pull out all the ones for students who did not start out in the program, and see if there are more errors."

After a few minutes spent silently doing this, we came up with twelve. Of those, a few seconds glance was enough to yield proof that five of them could not have gotten into the program with their grades. They were all athletes. One of these was Laurie Boone, who was only entering the program as a senior, and whose yearly grades never met the expected criteria. Again, I cursed by distraction, I had barely given any thought to her presence in my class, though I could think of no other student who had entered the program so late.

"I have no idea what to say. But this must have something to do with why Dolores gave this to us. Teachers do not have access to a student's overall transcript, only what grades we give."

"Who does?"

"Anyone administrative has a log-in to the administrative network; the guidance department as well."

I thought for a moment.

"And secretaries, because they are the ones who actually generate a lot of the reports."

We sat for a few minutes. At another time I would have found our collective silence amusing, but I at least was quiet because I was disturbed. Even the suggestion of academic wrongdoing on the part of a colleague made me uncomfortable. And something was wrong here.

"You need to get going," Noah pointed to the clock, which was about to chime noon. I did need to meet up with Mark and Ginny and get set for the exams.

"Why don't I take the folder? You will have your hands full with the summer reading tests, while all I have to do is proctor the second one. Let me see if I can find any other patterns or mistakes in this."

Why not? I thought to myself. I did have a tremendous amount of work to get through, in a very short amount of time. There was also the added consideration of classes, which began tomorrow and for which I had had no real equivalent for the past eight months.

"Great. We can speak about it later."

"Knock, knock," Ginny said, neither knocking nor pausing as she entered my room. Her immediate grin suggested an obvious misunderstanding of what she was looking at. No doubt Noah and I looked a bit nonplussed, and perhaps guilty but she could not know the real cause. I trusted her ethics completely, just not her ability to remain silent about the ethical breaches of others.

"Ginny. Hey. Do you know Noah Stabler?" I let Noah chat with Ginny while I straightened out my desk and put the Honor's folder into his bag.

We walked out into the hall together, and separated at the staircase. I said nothing more to Noah but no doubt looked like I wanted to.

Grabbing Ginny as we descended the stairs, I hissed, "one word, and I will kill you." He would not have heard me but could not miss her cackling laughter.

"Wow, Ms. Lake. You're here."

I smiled at Sam Janakowski, an extraordinary tall basketball player and member of my senior Honors class. The underclassmen exams had gone on without a hitch. My boxes of journals had already been stowed away in the trunk of my car by Frankie DiMeo. Neither of us had much time for chatter and I was simply glad he returned my keys before running to find the classroom of his own test.

"How are you Sam? I am expecting fine things from your essay. All of your essays."

I smiled, knowing how well Sam responded to positive affirmation. She did seem pleased at my compliment but troubled by the number of essay questions evidently on the exam. The Honors seniors had been assigned four works to read over the summer so I was not sure how she could have expected much less from the test.

Continuing to stand, as students filtered in and dropped off their journals, I reminded Scott Pearson to let DiMeo take the box away when the test was completed. I shook my cane at him as a reminder that I could not take the box myself. He nodded at me vaguely and returned to the task of lining up exams, test paper, and scrap neatly on his desk. Enduring an unbidden image of what Mrs. Pearson's home life must be like, I went to my classroom to begin to tackle the sophomore journals.

"That should be it, Frankie. Thanks again."

The journals would be making their temporary home in the trunk of my car, as I would carry into my home only the ones I honestly intended to grade that evening. Of course were I to be even more honest with myself, my intentions never matched my accomplishments where grading was concerned. I was worried my average would sink further now that I had the additional responsibilities of steady workouts and physical therapy. I had thus far found it impossible to not be exhausted after both.

"No problem, Ms. Lake. Hey, you do the senior test, right?"

I nodded my head cautiously, worried the defensive lineman was angered by something in the test I designed.

"I think I did alright," he said, mimicking my head nod, but with much more vigor.

"That's wonderful, Frankie."

"Yeah, I read the books this time—"

He stopped then, to glance at me, but I showed no reaction, because I felt none. At one point or another they all attempted to get by without reading the books. Some occasion usually arose, like this one, or worse, a failing grade, that taught them the error of their ways.

"And," Frankie continued, "my dad said I could go to Florida with the rest of the team if I kept my grades up."

"Florida?" I asked, while I rooted around in my purse for my house keys, so that I could transfer them to my pocket for easier removal later. Balancing life with an unbalanced leg and a cane required advanced planning.

"Yeah, Coach got us this trip for Columbus Day weekend. We'll see a Jaguars game and watch them practice first."

"Thanks great, hon." I assumed the Jaguars were a football team, though I supposed in October, baseball might still be a possibility. I was more ignorant on sporting matters than I should be, considering how popular a topic it was for many of my students.

"You got everything, Ms. Lake? I got to go lift."

"I am fine, Frankie. Lift away. I will see you tomorrow."

I got into my car quickly, hoping I was not embarrassed to be seen struggling and drove away thinking about Florida. I wondered just how Coach Brown argued that a trip to see a professional sporting event was a pedagogically sound choice at the start of the school year. There were several seniors on the team, like Frankie, and their time would be better served visiting college campuses in preparation for the decisions they would be making in the coming months.

I was vaguely troubled by the enormity of the scholar athlete's commitments. There were morning workouts, as well as evening practices, nighttime and weekend games, to say nothing of their school work. But perhaps all this effort better prepared them for their complex adult lives?

I had no idea, frankly, having not been pressed into any work or clubs as a teen. There were now days I felt barely adequate to accomplishment one task, let alone many, and I wondered if there wasn't a connection.

That night, it took four trips back and forth to my car to both bring in and return graded journals. The elation I felt to have completed two classes worth almost offset my fatigue at having done so.

Chapter 3

"I want this to be cut, and I do the leg lifts, but..."

"Hi, Mary. How are you feeling today? Did you get those M.R.I. results yet?"

"You like this color? I spilled coffee on my other scrubs and this was all they had..."

Like T.S. Eliot had once said of riding in an underground train, where you could be conscious but conscious of nothing, I generally let the conversations at physical therapy flow around me, hearing them but not really paying attention.

After my workout, I went to one of the five back tables to receive electronic stimulation to my ankle and knee, and wait for Tim, the therapist, to treat me. These tables were each only separated by a curtain.

There was always noise around me, disembodied voices and snippets of conversation. Having more than a decades' worth of experience ignoring noise when I needed to, I blocked out most of what I heard. Sometimes though, as when someone talked loudly on their cell phone, I was hostage to their half of the conversation.

Eight months into my recovery it was arguably no longer necessary for me to attend physical therapy. A gym membership could provide much of the same benefits. But I had come to rely on seeing Tim Boone three times a week. It was comforting to talk to someone about my injury and pains that reacted to my descriptions dispassionately, and offered helpful advice

Tim was always positive but also realistic. He had recently begun to help me weigh the pros and cons of additional surgery to relieve some pain in my ankle and knee joints. But he took the time to hear my worries and address them. Protracted conversations were virtually impossible with my surgeon, so I appreciated the way

Tim never seemed to rush me, no matter how many other patients were waiting.

"And how is my favorite patient?" Tim came from behind my curtain with even more of a jaunt than usual. He was a distinctly mobile man, always bouncing, snapping, jingling, and tapping. He would never take anyone by surprise.

"Not bad," I equivocated, "though the swelling is much worse since I went back to school."

"Yes, we were expecting that. You need to find time to rest and elevate it during the day."

As he spoke he took the electrodes from my knee and ankle and began to massage my calf. His fingers were like vices and I braced myself for each touch.

"I will. Regular classes only just started so I will get into a better routine."

"Yes, Laurie is thrilled to be in your class."

Tim began to flex my ankle and rotate my foot in all directions. I thought briefly about the impact of teaching Tim's daughter. I also recalled that she was new to the Honor's Program and was one of the five students whose grades suggested they should not be in it at all.

"Yes and I was surprised to see her in the Honor's Program. Not too many transfer in as seniors."

Actually, in all of the years I had been a teacher in the program, no senior had. Laurie had apparently set some type of precedent that had neither been noted nor wondered at, as far as I could tell.

"We finally convinced her to join. She had been asked after freshman year but didn't want to leave her friends." Tim shook his head at the peculiar priorities of the young.

If that was indeed true, and I was not sure how it could be, given what I had seen, I had an idea of who was responsible for Laurie's sudden change of heart. But teenagers will allow their friends, and sometimes by default, their teachers, to know things about themselves they would not dare tell their parents. I knew Laurie was dating Johnny Marchiano but that did not mean her father did, so I opted to keep my council.

"Well senior year is a great one for all St. Augustine's students. We do a lot of work to both prepare them for the college process and their first year of college."

"That's great. I was completely clueless during my freshman year. Of course I went to a boy's high school in Brooklyn. Class was barely important enough to get me out of my co-ed dorm."

I laughed. "Where did you go?"

"Up the road, SUNY Binghamton. I did my graduate work at N.Y.U"

"You did? We followed the same path, but in reverse. I was N.Y.U. for undergrad and then I came up here."

"Have to be very different years," he said with an exaggerated grimace and gesture toward his thinning hair.

I waved that comment off. I had no idea how old Tim was but, hair aside, he was in excellent shape, as I imagined a physical therapist had to be. He was fairly tall, with a waist line and shoulders that suggested regular workouts, not just enviable metabolism.

"Tim you look amazing and probably don't have a half gallon of ice cream for every day of the working week."

He shook his head, dear man, like I was exaggerating.

"I guess I do watch what I eat, maybe more now. I have also been doing this new circuit workout. It's called Lunacy, and it is. Forty minutes, no breaks, with weights, cardio, calisthenics. I hadn't done a jumping jack since grammar school and they really do get your heart rate up when you do a hundred of them in a row."

"I can imagine," I said, even though I could not. We were only just ready to have me try balancing on one leg, while I clutched a table. The impact of a jumping jack made me sick to even contemplate.

"When do you have the time?" I asked, curious. I had been in sessions with Tim early in the morning and, as now, the evenings. I also knew he saw homebound patients a few times a week.

"My only untapped opportunity is really early in the morning. Coach Brown actually lets me use the facilities at your school. There is some team practice there almost every day. I can get in, work out, and be home and showered by the time Laurie gets up at seven."

I just grimaced, as he had moved up my leg to grasp my knee and squeeze.

"Yo."

I did not, nor would ever, say that word. It had emitted from behind the curtain to my left, and was clearly a male voice. It was not Brian, the college aged barista from the local coffee shop. I had ordered enough devilish concoctions from his store to recognize the sound of his voice, plus I had already heard his high pitched desire for some muscle definition in his leg.

"Excuse me a minute," Tim said, already on the move. "You can work on your new leg lifts. Use your abs."

"Sure," I answered, smiling. Clearly all of my protestations that I had no abs had been for naught. Since Tim was an optimist I tried to be one as well, and did ten lifts with each leg. I didn't think holding my breath was the same thing as tightening my abs, but it would have to do for now.

I heard Tim and the other man whispering, but oddly heard nothing of their content. My attention had only been drawn by the act of whispering, otherwise I would have paid no mind. Tim's voice was usually on the louder side of loud and I had to assume their discussion contained some information not for the women around them to hear.

A few minutes later, having done another set of lifts to cement my awesomeness, Tim returned. Behind him walked the man I had dubbed "Angry Cop," mainly because the only things I knew about him were that he was a state trooper and that he was apparently angered by everything. I had rarely seen a grown person so vexed by inanimate things, especially innocuous things like exercise balls and giant rubber bands.

49

"How did you do?" Tim asked me, bouncing and booming again.

"Twenty of each," I said, proudly.

"That's great. Why don't I stretch out your back and we can call it a night. You need your strength to grade those summer reading tests."

"You know it," I said, rolling on to my stomach in a non-fluid set of motions.

I chose to believe that Tim was merely an attentive listener to my complaints and was not obliquely referring to his daughter's exam, which I had not even graded. I would rather avoid setting a precedent of talking about her performance here, though I would gladly take his phone calls or answer his emails while I was at work.

By the time we were done and I had tied my shoe, Tim had moved on to Brian and some complex discussion of basketball. Tying one sneaker had alerted me to the need to retie the other, so I sat down outside the reception area in time to actually observe Angry Cop smiling. The shock was great enough to make me glad that I was already seated.

His ACL knee surgery had brought him to Tim's about a month after I had begun attending. I was still using a walker then and had to be taken to therapy by my mother or father, who had stayed with me during the first months of my recovery. Angry Cop had rebuffed all of their attempts at conversation and I had not even tried myself, despite he and I being the most consistent patient the other saw. He could be as rude as he felt to me, but my parents were nothing but kind. I had written him off as a completely lost cause as a result of his disdain.

The minutes on Tim's implements of torture certainly went a bit faster with someone to chat with and luckily, Angry Cop's attitude was the exceptional one. I had passed many a kindly conversation with the other attendees at therapy, as we were inclined to more sympathy for each other than most physically well people could muster.

"Nah, I'm telling you, I can get them, no problem."

Angry Cop had spoken, obviously not to me, still obscured by the machines outside the reception area, but to Audrey, the young receptionist and aid.

"Yeah," she said in what sounded like more of a non-answer than an actual question. Her head was still angled toward her computer screen and not facing Angry Cop. He had a monotonous, low drawl that made me wonder how she even heard him. Audrey asked me to repeat almost everything I said, and I generally suffered from the heightened projection of a teacher of teenagers.

"Yeah, you've seen Boone's wife. How do you think she got that way so fast?"

Audrey did swivel her head towards Angry Cop when he said that and I was all but forced to wonder what they saw when they viewed Tim's wife. I had never met her and was now left with a puzzle, which annoyed me to no end. It was akin to seeing bumper stickers or vanity license plates that clearly had some meaning, but only sent me scrambling for guesses.

"Friday?"

I stood and asked this of Audrey, as more of a confirmation than anything else. I never missed therapy. She looked startled by my sudden appearance but Angry Cop did not even glance up from his cell phone. Had he been using it while speaking to Audrey? This was an abhorrent habit to me and I wouldn't be surprised if he did it with regularity. I walked around him to reach my cane, pretending he was not even there.

Later I heated up some sausage and bean soup and I settled down to grade a few journals with my dinner. Eating while grading was a terrible habit I could not break. I rarely minded living alone, but meal time seemed so institutional if I did not have something to distract me. This seemed a bit more productive than the television. Nevertheless it was an awkward conversation when a student received a paper that was tinged with mustard or speckled with gravy.

With Tim's words about his daughter in my mind, I had taken in the pile of journals that included hers and her boyfriend's. The first book that the senior Honors class had been assigned was George Eliot's *The Mill on the Floss*. It was an evocative but heavy novel of stunted desires and transgression. Though it would be rewarding, it was also incredibly depressing to read.

Immediately Laurie's journal entries raised my suspicions, especially in contrast to her writings on the other three works. It behooved every English teacher to familiarize themselves with the available on line study guides for the works we assigned. Laurie's journal entries, which were supposed to be chapter based reactions were curiously cogent summaries that also featured assessments of imagery, tone, and symbolism, each time and always in that order. Her later entries had no such professional organization and grasp of literary devices.

Telling myself that I routinely performed the same investigation with every student whose contributions I doubted, I went to my computer. Plagiarism was not a common occurrence in my classes, but it did happen. Interestingly, the inundation of internet based sources made it both easier for a student to cheat and easier for their teacher to catch them. I simply typed one of the lines of Laurie's journal into a search engine and quickly learned which guide she had taken for her own.

On a hunch, I pulled out the journal of Laurie's new boyfriend, Johnny Marchiano, but quickly felt guilty for having done so. Johnny had been in the Honor's Program since he arrived at St. Augustine's. He was one of those curiously gifted students, who managed academic and extracurricular success with a job at his father's convenience store. He also possessed a humble nature that made it largely impossible for the students primed to be jealous of him, to actually manage it. I was always vigilant for signs that Johnny felt his responsibilities too keenly but he appeared content with his life.

Scanning through his journal entries on *The Mill on the Floss*, I quickly recognized his own terse style. Johnny did not identify with Maggie Tulliver's search for love and intellectual challenge but was interestingly disturbed by her duplicity. The writing was all his own and he had evidently done nothing to help with Laurie's assignment, which I was glad to see. Couples did not always view their sharing of work as cheating, considering how symbiotic their relationships could be.

I finished the entire set of journals and returned them to my car, still perturbed by Laurie's deception, if I could call it that. Given the remainder of her journal, there was no way anyone could have been tricked into thinking the plagiarized writing was hers. She had also clearly attempted to analyze the other assigned works, particularly the plight of Edna Pontellier, in *The Awakening*. Edna's struggle seemed to trouble her, as it usually did girls in the class. Most boys sited that novella as their least favorite but I continued to assign it year after year, more optimistic with literature than perhaps I was with life.

I was not sure how to proceed with the situation with Laurie. The department counted the journal as fifty percent of the overall summer reading exam. The exam itself then comprised twenty five percent of their overall first quarter grades. It was a serious enterprise here.

Laurie had effectively not completed a fourth of her journal assignment, having written her own entries for the aforementioned novels and the play, *Cat on a Hot Tin Roof*. She could still do respectfully on the overall test, provided her written exam was decent, and I only penalized her for the quarter of the journal she plagiarized, and not fail her for the entire thing. Should I void her entire journal for the one infraction? I did not believe so but was unsure where the school policy would fall in this particular case.

As luck would have it, Ginny called while I was eating my ice cream and mulling my options morosely. I explained the situation to her immediately, leaving out the identity of the student. Ultimately my decision would be my own but I was glad to have another voice weigh in, especially when that voice had double my experience.

"Just talk to her Addra. If she tried with all the other books and did well enough on her test, maybe she was just genuinely stumped and took too much from the guide. She could have been reading it to try and understand the damn book."

I was glad that Ginny had called.

"*The Mill on the Floss* is no walk in the park, remember. Just thinking about it makes me want to sit down and cry. That and *Jude the Obscure*."

I laughed. I loved that novel but it was as dark and complex as one could get.

"Don't forget *Ethan Frome*," I added.

"Uh, another one. We make high school students read a lot of depressing stuff."

"It's true but I think they are used to it. Think about it, the middle of every Disney film has the main character lost, orphaned, or punished."

Now it was Ginny's turn to laugh, which translated more as a snort over the phone.

"At least those all turn out in the end. Disney can make an optimist out of anyone. You cannot say the same for Thomas Hardy."

"But nobody did come," I quoted, "because nobody does; and under the crushing recognition of his gigantic error Jude continued to wish himself out of the world."

"Exactly. Though he may have had a point,"

"Uh-oh." I said, belatedly remembering that Ginny may have called for a purpose.

"I knew you were flying out of school to get to therapy, so I didn't get a chance to tell you. Sister went to Mark's office to tell him that Friday would be an excellent opportunity for us to return the summer reading exams."

"Friday? This Friday? But that's in less than two days!"

Ginny was a good enough friend that I did not have to worry about shrieking in her ear.

"Why is Friday an excellent opportunity? Why couldn't Monday be equally excellent? I need the weekend. Does she have any idea what she is asking?"

"No," Ginny interrupted. "She doesn't. She also doesn't care. Apparently some parents have called her directly to ask about when we are returning them. Knowing Mark, he probably forwarded her the calls, rather than deal with them himself."

"Ridiculous," I muttered, but the more charitable half of my brain was already reminded the other half of the delicate balance we in the private school arena had to find with the parents. They were essentially our customers, once removed.

"Of course Mark just agreed since his journals were done a few hours after the kids handed them in. It's easy when you are not burdened with actually reading them. He just checks how many pages they are."

My more charitable self also speculated that I would not have disagreed with Sister either and certainly not by arguing that the work was as yet incomplete. But Ginny needed to have at least one uninterrupted diatribe about Mark per day, and I had not seen her since Tuesday.

Eventually even she needed to breathe, so when she did I changed the subject by noting how much work I would have to try to get done in between classes tomorrow. Even as I said it, I knew it would prove impossible. So did Ginny.

"Sure. That won't be a problem at all," she said, bidding me a mirthful goodnight.

After one more scoop of ice cream and an aggressive bout of tooth brushing, I took myself to bed, newly determined that I would encounter no problems completing my grading tomorrow. I may have panicked in the moment, but if I were to be truthful with myself, I was not overly bothered by my current predicament. Compared to the months of significant fears and worries, to be back to my pre-accident form, with mountains of papers to grade, was wonderful. I went to bed the best way possible, utterly fatigued and with no dreams strong enough to wake me.

Chapter 4

"I am exhausted."

I made this announcement not really expecting an answer, but I did see a few nods as I entered the faculty room. I also saw some glares, having broken one of the commandments of the room. I had spoken when a student was still present. Today, Xavier Nantz, a junior of questionable motivation but kind enough impulses, was helping me. I was down to my last bin of summer reading tests, having already finished all the journals, save Laurie's. I still needed to make a decision there and quickly.

In normal circumstances I would simply finish grading them in my own room. But my leg ached even more than usual and I needed to rest and elevate it, as Tim had cautioned. To the faculty room, therefore, Xavier had to go.

"You are a prince," I told him with a grin, craning my neck a bit because he was so tall.

Xavier just shook his head. "See you later, Ms. Lake." He ignored everyone else in the room.

"That boy sleeps in the library," Lucille Bartlett pronounced as soon as he had exited. She was the librarian, so I imagined she would know. Having no response to this, I attempted to divert attention.

"You want to help me grade these things? I have a dollar I could give you."

I was kidding, but would definitely ferret that dollar out of my purse if Lucille said yes.

"You are going to give me your whole salary, just for that?"

"No, maybe not my whole salary, but definitely the rest of my disability."

Lucille and I sighed at that statement, acknowledging the spirit of its truthfulness if not the letter. It had been Lucille, who still suffered the lingering effects of a hip replacement two years ago, who had recommended Tim Boone to me.

Though we had been chatting acquaintances more than actual friends, Lucille had been one of the first to visit me in the hospital. She came bearing her quadruple chocolate cookies, which were produced only at Christmas time. My nurse had come running in, disturbed by the spike in my heart rate, but the cost was worth it. Since then, Lucille had taken a decided interest in my health, and had come to visit two Sundays a month, cookies in hand each time.

"You need to elevate that leg," she said, pointing to the plump red sofa in the corner of the room. Sal had placed that comfortable monstrosity as far away from the door as possible, lest any visiting parent or alumni see it and assume what they should not.

"Don't I know it?" I grabbed a sheaf of papers and wobbled my way over to the sofa. My leg had a tendency to buckle when it was overtaxed and I was glad to make it to the ottoman style end piece of the sectional before that happened. I set my cell phone to act as an alarm, so I could return to the safety of my room before the student's stormed the halls. Thereafter I hunkered down with my red pen and some cautious optimism.

"Should I be worried you are ignoring me?"

I looked up, blinking and confused. I was ignoring no one, simply working. Since I was not through nearly enough essays, I tried to stem my irritation at Jeremy Wrobleski, who well knew how busy I was. That he would knowingly interrupt me summed up Jeremy's personality as well as anything else did.

"How are you Jeremy?"

"Oh, I am as right as rain, Addra and happy to see you resting. Every time I look out my window I see you hopping from place to place like a bunny."

"Well," I grimaced. "Not quite hopping."

There was just something that irked me about Jeremy. Perhaps it was only his word choice, which always seemed vaguely insulting, in ways you could never definitively prove.

I kept my eyes upon him as he began to talk, uninterrupted, about some topic doubtless only he cared about, but inside I was trying to determine what animal he would be, were I rude enough to assign him one to his face. If I were going to be a bunny, then he would be a walrus, a lumbering, blustering walrus, right down to the drooping mustache.

"...perhaps you know?"

"Um, no, not really," I hedged. With Jeremy, ignorance seemed a safer thing to plead than knowledge. Besides it was more politic than admitting I was paying no attention to what he said.

"Don't you believe someone must verify the truth of this?"

"The truth of what, exactly?"

Jeremy looked at me, slightly disappointed, which did not bother me at all.

"Why, Addra, whether or not your new English teacher is having an inappropriate relationship with a female student."

This was not at all what I expected him to say.

"Wait! What? What proof do you have?" I glanced around the faculty room, glad to see that no one paid us any mind.

"I have no proof, Addra, only the counsel of others." Jeremy leaned back in the sofa, crossing his legs in front of him, looking more calm than someone should, given our topic of conversation. Inside I seethed, since council was nothing but his code word for gossip.

"If you trust this council, shouldn't this conversation be between you and Sister, or Mark, at least?"

"We have not reached that point yet," he said slowly. "This is simply the fact gathering stage. I only wondered what you knew of the man."

My eyes narrowed, a condition I was finding more common since I had returned to this place. The fact gathering stage, Dolores had used the very same phrase when sharing potential wrong doing with me. When had I become the secret keeper of those above me?

"I know nothing of the man, Jeremy. But if you are intimating that something inappropriate is going on between him and a student you need to alert Sister."

Jeremy sat up.

"You are misunderstanding me, Addra. No one said anything inappropriate was definitely occurring. You have been alone too much, dear, and have lost the skill of conversation."

I felt a burning sensation creep its way up from my chest. Inappropriate had been Jeremy's word, not mine. But I was flummoxed over how to respond, as I usually was when someone was deliberately snide.

"No, Jeremy," I said, with a sickly smile, "I have not lost my skill of conversation, just my patience for games."

"Have a nice day, Ms. Lake."

At hearing this, I turned slowly from my computer and large screen. The final bell had rung and most of the sophomores already knew to run from the room as though it were on fire. Here stood Katie, a small girl with fine, red hair.

"You have a wonderful night, sweetie. And thank you again for your comments about the Revolutionary War."

We were reading some of the letters between John and Abigail Adams, and Katie had provided some impressive detail about the general treatment of women in that era. I looked forward to having her in class this year.

Giving me a small smile, she lurched from the room, her pink backpack extending alarmingly far from her body. Recalling the size of their literature text, I resolved to create more assignments that did not necessitate bringing it home.

This had been a difficult day to get through. I had not been able to shake the thinly disguised viciousness of Jeremy's comments and devoted too much time to wondering how I could have handled him better. I was no

60

fan of Ken Telford, but those were the sort of rumors that destroyed a career, even if they were false. And I was inclined to believe that Jeremy had no counsel and was playing a very different game with me.

He had already referenced watching me come up and down the main pathway, so it likely he had also seen Ken and Toni Anne. Their body language may well have raised his suspicions, and he invoked the idea of a student to trap me into revealing something about our colleagues. Just thinking that Jeremy may have seen me hiding behind that tree made me light headed.

And what did I know, really, about Ken and Toni Anne? I had seen them appearing quite friendly at the faculty meeting, but Joe and I would have appeared the same to another observer. Joe was also married while I was not, but I had never given the propriety of his friendship a single thought.

Ken and Toni Anne had seemed to arrive at school by the same car, but I had not actually seen either of them exit, merely heard two car doors slam while I was already on the path. It was entirely possible one had arrived by a separate car while I was already past view.

Still, I countered with myself, as I slowly completed the tasks of classroom clean up, had they been in the same car, they certainly had lingered for a while. In fact considering how timed their exits were to my vacating the parking lot it was hard to argue against the fact that they did not want to be seen together.

But I had seen them, and Ken at least was aware that I had. More worrisome was the fact that Sal had seen them too. At the very least something had made him curious and now he had ample reason to be suspicious. I did not think he would have spoken to Jeremy, but as a world class gossip, Jeremy could easily have gleaned what he wanted to know. I sighed. For all the stereotypes that attended teenagers, I thought that many of the people who taught them showed greater propensities for backstabbing and innuendo.

Once the blinds had been raised half way and the desks straightened to the best of my ability, I kicked the garbage pail out into the hall with my good leg. I was not sure which member of the football team was coming for me this afternoon but we would be doing a bit more work.

In my haste to get away from Jeremy I had neglected the bin of tests in the faculty room. It needed to be stowed back in my classroom for easy distribution tomorrow. I still needed to complete a set of essays, tabulate the combined grades, and enter them both on the tests and in my old fashioned grade book. Then I planned to arrive extremely early tomorrow morning to place each student's test booklet inside of their journal. This way everyone would receive their full test back with the overall grade concealed. My consideration for their privacy was largely wasted as several students per class would still call out their own grade, whether it was good or bad. Actually, the worse the grade the more likely the student was, if a boy, to call it out, with some twisted sense of pride.

"Hey." It was Noah and I had chewed off most of my lipstick hours ago.

"What are you up to?"

"Hi," I managed, bemoaning too my tendency to run fingers through my hair when stressed. I could actually feel it standing up and away from my head like an unkempt mane. I had managed to be a bunny and a lion in one day. Why couldn't he have stopped by in the morning, before class, when I still had the possibility of looking collected and unstained?

"I was just recalling a professor I had in college who returned tests in grade order, while commenting on the grades as he did so."

Noah's eyes drifted to the bins of tests I had lining the window sill.

"I walk around the lab to give each paper back. With the round tables, it seems the easiest way."

Pleased he had followed my unspoken train of thought so easily, I asked,

"Have you settled in well? I haven't seen you." I spoke, hoping I did not sound too eager to see him.

"Yes, and you were right. I really am enjoying the students. Plus they mostly start off finding physics intimidating, that guarantees me their attention."

"I know," I grinned, "and I have always been jealous. Students and parents always take science and math more seriously than the liberal arts. No matter how doctrinaire he may be, Scott Pearson gets the parents to go along with everything he says." Pearson was the antiquated chairperson of the math department. He would have the students using abacuses instead of calculators if he could.

"And the kids always have graph paper," Noah responded.

"And pencils."

We both smiled at each other allowing the conversation to reach that awkward point where one topic is ended but none had yet taken its place.

"About those five new Honors students," he began, as Frankie DiMeo burst into the room with not even the pretense of knocking.

"Yo, Ms, Lake," he said to me, giving Noah the curious chin raise that was typical of young men these days. He was never a serious boy but seemed particularly kinetic for him.

"What are you so giddy about, on a Thursday?" I asked.

"Mr. Telford gave back the summer reading tests today and I got a 90. I was late getting here because I had to call my dad."

"So you are all set for Florida?" I asked, firmly trying to focus on Frankie and not on my burgeoning anger at Ken Telford for getting all his papers graded before I did. Had Mark been counseling him on how to grade without actually grading?

Frankie didn't sense anything was wrong and simply grinned.

"All set."

For a moment I was afraid we were about to high five each other and his slope shouldered strength would send me stumbling, but he only reached behind me for my bag.

"Before we head out Frankie, would you mind getting the last bin of tests from the faculty room and bringing them back up here? I'll go with you."

"Sure," he said, grabbing my book bag anyway and giving Noah another chin raise in farewell.

"Hey, this is light," he exclaimed from the doorway, swinging the bag with one finger.

"I am walking home tonight," I said by way of explanation.

"Why don't you wait downstairs with your bag, Ms. Lake? I can stay here and lock up after Frankie brings the bin up, unless you need help, Frankie?"

"Nah," Frankie's snort was not derisive towards Noah, only to the notion that he needed help carrying one crate of papers. I could have climbed into said crate and Frankie would still lift it with one hand.

"Thank you, Mr. Stabler," I said, exiting after Frankie. "We can talk about the Honors Program tomorrow?"

"Sure," Noah nodded. "If you have the time."

I supposed he was aware that I was not as caught up with my grading as the alacritous Mr. Telford. How could Ken be teaching, moderating two clubs, acclimating to the school, and conducting a clandestine affair while still having time to get all his grading done? Clearly all of my early attempts at charity had fled and I was utterly and irrationally miffed.

After holding the door open for Frankie, who entered and exited the faculty room without incident, I awaited his return with my bag at my feet. When he came bounding door the stairs I was still attentive enough to catch the keys he lobbed at me. I do not care how old a person may be, missing an easy catch like that would have been embarrassing.

"Awesome," he said, grabbing my bag.

"I can carry this to the alley. You are going home that way, right?"

"I am, hon, but you go ahead to practice. This is light and I walk a lot slower than you do. You did wonderfully on your exam, Frankie, congratulations."

"Thanks, Ms. Lake," he threw over his shoulder as he bounded out the door.

I waited a few minutes before I followed. Noah never came down the stairs.

Once outside I stood taking a few calming breathes while I debated which way I would walk to the alley. Hiking across the lawn, I would only need to walk past the track and out. The lawn was not well manicured but landscaped with tall trees that predated anything else on campus. Their roots caused the ground to be uneven and I was sure the wet leaves and decaying crab apples would also prove to be obstacles for me. I was somewhat clumsy at the best of times, and my mangled leg made me a hazard to myself.

Still, in some ways this was the easier route and the one where I would be least likely to run into anyone. If I proceeded down the path to the parking lot, then over to the athletic complex, I would have to go past the equipment and weight rooms, the offices, the football field, baseball diamond and then the track. I would be walking on cleaner surfaces, but much of my trip would be in the wrong direction. There was also the added issue of Jeremy Wrobleski. I now knew that he spent a good deal of time looking out his wide office window and would be feeling his eyes upon me whenever I was on the main path.

Shuddering a bit, I turned towards the lawn. I would simply be extra careful and not let my mind or eyes wander from the path before me. The autumn sun was already setting and I knew I would enjoy the smells of the waning day. It was cool enough for some lucky people on 10th street to use their wood burning stoves and the scent of this filled me with more calm.

I focused on nothing but ensuring my safe walk and soon reached the entrance to the alley, which was bordered by low concrete walls on both sides. It was only a quarter mile in length and would let out at the top of the 10th avenue cul de sac. The seniors who wrangled parking spots on the street came this way, as did any walker, like me, who lived east ward of the school.

Apparently, one also came here for a smoke, if the cigarette butts that littered the walk way were any indication. This issue arose every few years, and I reminded myself to speak to the Dean of Students, Linda Mullen. Unless you were actually standing on one end of the alley or the other, it was obscured from view, so a teacher would have to be posted right here to effectively patrol.

Peering more closely in the declining light, I looked at what appeared to be tire marks on the ground, as well as some scrapes along the concrete wall that could have been made from a car mirror. Good Lord, I thought, aghast. Were kids daring each other to drive down this alley? I thought about the athletic complex as I resumed my walk.

There was a parking lot behind the baseball field, which essentially served as a lot for spectators of all our sporting events. That lot was accessible by 9th street and I supposed a car could, in theory, be driven behind the fields to the alley way. But why would anyone do this, save for a dare?

I was mostly troubled because the athletic coaches and Nick Morrison, the director, were supposed to supervise the kids at all times. Did this prove that someone was not doing their job? Or was I so focused on the potential for vehicular danger that I was making a serious situation where one did not exist?

My brain was crying out for my cozy little house and some hot food. I no longer wanted to think about the myriad of school problems that had suddenly come my way. And, I reminded myself, I had not spoken to Laurie Boone privately, since she had a soccer game to get to immediately after class.

Exiting the alley, I walked to my right, surprised that Mitch and Wanda were not on their stoop across the street. The cul de sac was lined with cars that most likely belonged to students still on campus. I felt much more sure-footed walking on this well kept street, where most homeowners raked their leaves multiple times a day.

I stopped in front of Mr. Delgado's house, feeling suddenly strange. It was then that I realized: I had walked through the alley without my accident being foremost on my mind.

On that night, the police speculated, I had come out of the alley way and walked to my right, like I had just done. It had been late and the street was mostly empty of cars. But one speeding, horribly inattentive driver had tried to swing out of the cul de sac, overturned, and struck me, walking on the sidewalk.

The impact had sent me back several feet, landing in the clump of leaves and growth that bordered the alleyway. It had been a strangely foggy night, for late December. Mitch and Wanda Doyle had been visiting her sister, and it had actually been Mr. Delgado who discovered me, after coming out to investigate the noise.

Since then, I had had a soft spot for Walter Delgado, though he was, without a doubt, the neighborhood crank. Looking at his terribly neat property, I recalled my earlier thought about him decorating for Halloween. The wires were no longer in evidence but he had not put his ladder away yet. It was another mystery.

Smiling slightly, I resumed my walk and was near the edge of his property when I heard his front screen door open.

"Mr. Delgado, how are you?"

"Fine, Addra, fine. I am glad you are here. Would you walk back to the hedge and then slowly walk back to where you are now?"

He went back inside without waiting for an answer.

I am sure I would have bided his request, had I not even been in his debt, since it was odd but hardly taxing. I retraced my steps over to the far side of his property then slowly proceeded to my earlier spot on the other end. I stood there, staring at his new, garish porch light until he reappeared.

"Come in," he commanded, again not waiting for me to respond. He let his squeaky screen door close behind him.

I chose not to over-think this increasingly strange encounter and opened his door myself. Inside was dark, save for one anemic lamp creating a pool of light in the corner of the front room. I followed a path through this, and past the kitchen, to an even darker room beyond.

Mr. Delgado was standing in front of a small television, playing black and white images.

"Look," he said, pointing. I moved in a bit further and squinted at the grainy image of myself, walking with the expected slow pace, past Mr. Delgado's house.

"Ah," I said, as I was wont to do when lacking anything else to say. His new porch light was evidently a camera, the wires had been needed to enable it, the ladder needed to reach it, and I needed to test its capability. But to what end?

"Mr. Delgado, why are you filming the street?"

"It's for the excrement."

"For the what?" I sputtered, caught between the desire to laugh and the desire to leave. For the past four days I had been surprised by the things people had said to me, but this was the worst.

Mr. Delgado leaned in closer and whispered. "The crap. The dog crap."

For a moment I just peered into the darkened room, hoping to find a medicine bottle that would either help explain this conversation or help end it, provided I could get the pills down his throat.

"They walk their dogs here, Addra, but they never pick up. Every morning, I have dog crap in my shoes. It has to stop. I can't watch all night, so I installed this."

"Ah, the dog crap," I said again, now with a bit more clarity. Mr. Delgado could certainly work on his communication skills, but his plan no longer seemed bizarre. Plenty of homeowners have cameras installed, for various reasons. I was also no stranger to the unexpected gifts that dog owners occasionally left on my lawn.

68

Though I had never thought to be as bothered as Mr. Delgado, who was I to judge? He took great pride in the neatness of his property. He had also set up his camera well. It was wide enough to reveal the entire sidewalk in front of his house as well as a tiny corner of the alley.

"Don't tell anyone," he commanded and dismissed me at once.

I assured him that I would never possess the proper words to describe this interlude and left for the relative calm of paper grading. By the time I reached my own walk way it was too dark to see what lay amongst the leaves. But I did check my shoes at the door, suspicion, like the common cold, was catching.

When earliest morning dawned I hauled myself out of bed and to my coffee. I had had nightmares but was glad to suffer ones not accident related. Mr. Delgado figured prominently in them.

Without giving myself time to wonder if I could get my work done in time, I downed a yogurt, splashed myself up in the shower, and pulled out of my drive by 6:15. Considering my recent issues with attention, I had already verified three times that the remaining set of papers were in my bag.

As I turned from Mayflower Road into the lot, I noted that I had beaten both Sister Paul and Dolores Donovan. Scott Pearson's car was here as was Sal's old truck. Sal arrived early by virtue of his job while I was secretly convinced Scott just never left. It was 6:22, by my watch.

There was one other car in the lot, closest to the Athletic complex and far away for any teacher who wanted to get to the academic building quickly.

"Not again," I muttered, turning away. I had no time to play chicken with Toni Anne and Ken. Grabbing my bag and cane I proceeded to walk towards the path before stopping. The car across the lot was not Ken's green hatchback, but it did look familiar. Squinting, while reminding myself that I really needed new contacts, I realized it must be Tim Boone's car. I had arrived early enough to interrupt his crazy workout. Craning my head a bit, I also noted that there was no noise. The football team must have the rare morning off from practice.

Delighted that I could say hello to Tim and feel good about the walk over to the weight room, I stowed my bag back in the car. I would just be a few minutes and would welcome chatting with someone unconnected to the school. My steps only faltered when I remembered I still had come to no decision about his daughter's plagiarized journal, and Tim was sure to ask.

At that moment, Sal exited the squat, brick building that held the weight room, equipment lockers, and athletic offices. He stumbled, an empty black garbage bag fluttering in his hand.

"Sal?" I called. His body language spoke of distress, even from across the expanse of concrete. I quickened my pace as much as I could to bridge the distance between us.

Before I had even arrived at his side, I heard Sal begin to mutter.

"He was already here. He was already here."

"Sal?" I called to him again, and reaching his side, pulled on his arm, to steady both of us.

"What is wrong?" His eyes were not fully focused on me and I was becoming horribly afraid. I felt my heart begin to thud and choke me.

"The doc is dead."

Tim was not a doctor but I knew immediately who he meant. Struggling to keep calm though my tears were already gathering, Sal and I spoke at the same time.

"You have to go call the police, Sal. I left my cell phone in my car."

"I need to find Sister."

He turned to run towards the Towers, before I could tell him that Sister had not arrived yet. Praying that Sal would call the police I turned towards the weight room, petrified at what I would find. I had no strength to move a grown man, nor any clear knowledge of how to help Tim if he had suffered a heart attack or something similar. But just the thought that he may still be alive, moved my feet without care for pain or falling.

Three things were clear when I entered the weight room and saw Tim, blood spattered, on the floor. He was not alive. I could not help him. And his death had not come naturally.

Since there was nothing I could do for my friend now, I just stood there, waiting with him, until the sounds of sirens pulled me out into the burgeoning light.

Chapter 5

The small conference room in the Towers, like most of its rooms, featured wide, leaded windows. As a room at the front corner of the second floor, I could see all the activity on the path and the parking lot beyond it.

The patrolmen who had earlier arrived with their sirens blaring had hustled me out of the weight room, and proceeded to check the entire building, apparently in search of Tim's killer. I had waited with him long enough to note the blood stained bar bell that lay at his side but had never considered that the killer could still be there. Faced with the enormity of his death I had not yet spared a moment of thought for the person who took his life.

Flexing my stiff leg a few times, I turned now to glance behind me. Sal was seated at one end of the rectangular table that dominated the room. He clutched a paper cup of coffee and was staring into it, as though hypnotized.

Scott Pearson was stodgily grading homework at the table's other end, thereby cementing my belief that something was truly wrong with him. As the only other person on campus when the body was discovered, an officer had evidently fetched Scott from his tiny, third floor office and told him to wait here. I could scarcely imagine a focus so single minded that a person would think to take along busy work when informed by the police that a murder had just been committed a few yards away.

Of course I was most likely mistaken to think the police ready to declare Tim a murder victim, but I knew what I saw. His body had been resting against an exercise bike, clear across the room from the case that held the bar bells. There was no other way for that weight to have half obliterated his face than to have had it raised against him, many times, in violence.

I shuddered again and focused upon my breathing. Not even the sight of my own mangled leg, which I had insisted upon seeing in the hospital, was as horrifying as the sight of Tim's broken body. It was also wrong of me to have described him as resting, for he had lay twisted and spasmodic. Had his last moments been filled with fear, shock, and pain? I was haunted by this thought.

Some deep recess of my brain still held on to the sense memory of being struck and thrown by the car. It was a sickening jolt that still returned to me, many times, in my dreams. And I was having difficulty now separating my own experience with physical violence from Tim's. Though mine had been accidental while his had to be deliberate, the people who had hurt us were out there and Tim had lost his life to serve the whim of his killer.

The enormity of this menace, in part, explained my utter breakdown in the parking lot, after the police had escorted me away from Tim. I had openly sobbed for a while, with ragged, painful breathes. My shaking caused my cane to fall away from me and was picked up by a young female officer, who looked distressed at my reaction.

Another officer had consulted with the newly arrived Sister Paul, and I was brought to this conference room. I may well have given way to more despondency if Sal and Scott had not followed me here. Their presence was steadying if not actually comforting.

I also understood why we were really here. As the only potential witnesses, the police would want to speak to us and no doubt wish to keep us from speaking to any of the other faculty now beginning to arrive.

From my vantage point, I had already witnessed Sister Paul and Dolores walk up the path with their secretaries, Ginny, and the chairperson of the History department, Elizabeth Maccabe. They entered the Towers, below me, while the other members of the faculty were being herded up the path in the opposite direction, into the academic building. I imagined that the kitchen staff was also being attended to, out of my sight.

Looking down at my watch I was surprised to see that it was 7:14. The early bird students would be arriving soon and I had no idea what that would mean. Thinking about the students made me think of Laurie Boone.

Then my mind drifted, unaccountably, to the littlest freshmen in my homeroom and I began to cry quietly.

"Mr. Vacarro?" The door had opened and the same officer who had led each of us here had arrived to take Sal elsewhere.

"Why don't you come too, Ms. Lake? Detective Lawson will see you in Sister Paul's office."

I walked around the table, surreptitiously wiping my face with my good hand. I briefly considered saying something to Scott as I left, but did not, doubting he would even take note of his solitude when we were gone.

Though quiet, Sal and I walked side by side, he no doubt slowing down for my sake. We took separate directions in the open area where the secretaries worked, as he was destined for Dolores' office and a Detective other than Lawson. As I made my way I heard the faint hum of voices and even believed I could detect Ginny's particular timber. We had taught in adjoining rooms before she was gifted with the larger one on the first floor, so I could well recognize her voice from behind walls.

Steeling myself, as I did any time I entered Sister Paul's office, I walked in.

"Ms. Lake?" A short man stood from behind Sister's desk. He wore a blue suit that immediately brought Sister to mind and I was suddenly struck by their eerie similarity. Detective Lawson also seemed to wear an expression of bland equanimity that I knew must belie a sharp mind.

"I am Detective Gene Lawson, of the Broome County police department. Are you feeling better?"

I was fairly certain Detective Lawson had not yet arrived when I had my little breakdown, which meant that I had subsequently become a topic of conversation. My face was burning so much as I sat that I did not even answer him right away. If I wanted to prove myself a complete flake I was doing a fine job.

"Yes. I'm sorry. But it was such a shock to see Tim. He was my physical therapist and," I hesitated here before deciding to continue.

"I was hit by a car in December, a hit and run. My emotions have gotten the better of me sometimes, since then."

He smiled at me, in a peculiarly distant way, and I was once again struck by his similarity to Sister Paul. I was also struck by how my statement could be misinterpreted as a confession, if someone were on the lookout for one.

"Yes, Sister Paul was quite concerned for you. I assume the driver is still at large?"

It was my turn to answer in the affirmative, sorry now to have broached the subject. I had worked hard to forget that I most likely lived in the same town as the person who had struck me and left me for dead. And now I lived in the same place as the person who had beaten Tim to death. Both thoughts were horribly disquieting.

Belatedly, I returned my attention to Detective Lawson, who was speaking.

"...Sister said you are not usually here so early."

"Ah, no. I am not."

My worry at being mistaken for a suspect increased ten-fold, but I was dogged in my attempt to remain calm, having already lost it once today.

"Sister just decided Wednesday that my department's summer reading exams should be returned today. I was—am—behind in grading them and got here early to finish."

The detective wrote something down, but did not speak, and excellent practice I soon discovered if you wanted the other person to continue talking.

"The exams included a journal component and I wanted time to place each student's essay test inside their journal so that I could pass back one item to each student and conceal their grades."

I took a deep breath and pursed my lips shut before I could tell him what books each grade read and how sloppy most of their penmanship was.

"And what time did you arrive?"

"6:22." I answered promptly, though perhaps too much so, considering Lawson's quickly raised eyebrows. Another long winded answer seemed appropriate.

"It is somewhat a campus legend that Sister Paul and Dolores Donavan, the vice principal, compete to arrive the earliest to school, so I was surprised to have beaten both of them."

"Anything else surprise you when you arrived?"

"No," I said slowly, giving his question thought. "Scott Pearson was already here but that's no surprise. He always gets here at the crack of dawn."

"When you say he was here, did you actually see him or just his car?"

"Just his car. I have no reason to ever go to the math office."

I hoped I did not over-emphasize the word ever, but I did make it a policy to avoid Scott when I could.

"Anyone else?" This time I was prepared for the Detective's response and answered accordingly.

"I also saw Sal Vacarro's truck, as I would expect to. Then I noticed Tim's car at the far end of the lot, but I did not realize yet that it was his. I took my book bag out of my car and started walking up the path to the academic building."

"Where were you going?" He interrupted again.

"To my classroom."

"And that is…?"

"On the second floor of the academic building, 2G."

"How would you get in at that time?"

"Sal opens all the main doors at six, so the cafeteria people can get in. I have a classroom key, we all do."

Detective Lawson wrote something down in his pad. I could read upside down, another occasionally useful skill for a teacher, but Sister Paul's desk was simply too wide for me to even see his scrawl.

This questioning was having a strangely calming effect on me. Detective Lawson's style was mechanical enough that we had achieved a kind of rhythm: question, answer, clarification, and writing.

"Why didn't you go to your classroom?"

"Well, I had been wondering whose car that was and when I realized it was Tim's I decided to go and say hi."

"How did you know it was his car?"

"I go to physical therapy three times a week, and have since January. You have to walk through the parking lot to get into the building. His spot is marked."

I decided not to tell the detective how focused I had become on cars, especially the ones I passed while walking. I always knew when someone was behind the wheel, whether the car was running or not. And I practiced recognizing makes, models, colors, and even license plates. The psychologist I had seen for a while after the accident said this was my attempt to regain control in my life.

"And why would he be at your school, so early in the morning?"

"He had told me that he was working out here, I am not exactly sure when he started. Our football coach, Coach Brown had told Tim he could use the facilities."

"Strange he would come here when he could have used the equipment in his own office."

Lawson had more implied his question than asked it, but I answered anyway, seeing as it was my role to do so.

"Tim had told me that the program he was following was one of those really aggressive ones. The equipment in his office is more designed for people recovering from injury."

I had been about to mention that the weights at physical therapy were not nearly as heavy looking as the one that had been used to kill Tim, but luckily stopped myself in time.

"Is it Coach Brown's right to invite people to use the school's facilities?"

Detective Lawson's voice and face still remained passive but the question was a pointed one. I began to worry for Coach Brown and to wonder if Sister Paul had even been aware of this arrangement.

"I am not really sure Detective. The academic and athletic sides of things are mostly kept separate. I only knew about Tim because of my relationship with him outside of school."

Realizing that that did not sound quite right, I tried again.

"I mean, knowing him as my physical therapist, in his office."

"Yes, Sister Paul also mentioned that her secretary saw Mr. Boone, in his office."

Again, it seemed that Detective Lawson had asked another 'non-question' question and a slightly mocking one at that. I was beginning to feel as my students must, with my frequent use of 'non-answer' answers. I considered those teaching tools but was also growing aware of how annoying they could be.

"Yes, Bernadette saw Tim." I did not mention that I secretly believed all of Bernadette's ailments to be no more than ploys. The only other school secretary's work load had increased quite a bit since Bernie had begun to complain of neck and back pain. More than once I had seen her thumb a magazine in the workout room, instead of doing her exercises.

"A guidance counselor here, Toni Anne Tancredi also goes to Tim, and our librarian, Lucille Bartlett, still sees him occasionally."

I let my mistake in tense stand uncorrected as I was growing more concerned that I was unintentionally suggesting suspects to Detective Lawson, who kept writing things down.

"Was Mr. Boone connected to the school in any other way?"

"Well, Sister Paul must have told you that his daughter is a senior here. Did you—was she home when you told…"

I hesitated but surely someone had informed Tim's wife that he was gone.

"Mrs. Boone has been informed but their daughter," here he paused to look at his notes, "Laurie, had already been picked up by her boyfriend. They apparently stop to get a few other friends as well. Rather than call her daughter, Mrs. Boone elected to wait for her here, so she can be the one to tell her."

"Thank God," I said I response, grateful that he had shared that much with me.

"Do you know Mrs. Boone?" Immediately we had gone back to our routine.

"No, I have never met her."

"But you teach Laurie?"

"Yes, but the school year has just started and she was never in my class before."

Abruptly, the detective stood, all but forcing me to do so as well.

"That should be it for now, Ms. Lake. The rest of the faculty has been told to wait in the faculty room. We would like to speak to you as a group once the students have been sent home. Please don't share details with anyone about how Mr. Boone died."

"Believe me; I won't be responsible for any gossip. But, Detective, this place is rife with it."

"I know. Sister Paul told me."

Briefly taken aback by that statement, I picked up my cane to navigate out of the office. I visited Sister Paul's office, at most, once a year, and was always struck by how austere it was, given her penchant for bright colors and plush furnishings elsewhere else on campus.

"Detective?" I asked before turning to leave. "Do you think the person who killed Tim is connected to St. Augustine's?"

I had tried to keep my voice from shaking but failed. Detective Lawson sighed before answering me.

"Ms. Lake, it is too early to know anything for certain. But we are dealing with a wide open campus, with several points of entry, none of which have video security. I cannot say the perpetrator is unconnected to the school anymore than I can say he or she is. But that is not very comforting." He sighed again.

"No, it isn't, Detective. But at least it's honest. Thank you."

I walked out steadily, slightly buoyed that Detective Lawson had not bothered to deny a murder had occurred. I could not allow myself to fall apart again as it was dawning on me that, until Tim's murderer was caught, I needed to be very careful.

"Addra," Ginny called from down the hall. Under normal circumstances she would never have raised her voice in the Towers. But under normal circumstances, we would be readying ourselves for homeroom, and not dealing with the immediate aftermath of a murder.

"My goodness, are you alright? Sister Paul said you discovered his body."

She pulled me into an awkward hug, my cane caught between us.

"Not exactly. Sal found him first."

Mindful to not be drawn into any specific questions, I said,

"I think we are to go to the faculty room to wait."

"Yes," Ginny agreed, taking my arm.

"Dolores and the Dean are personally shepherding the students into the cafeteria for now. Sister Paul got the police to move their squad cars into the sports lot, so no one would see them."

We walked downstairs and out into the sun. I needed to take a minute before going into the faculty room so we sat upon a stone bench. I had been saying frantic prayers for Tim and his family ever since stumbling upon him in the weight room, but I also said one prayer of gratefulness now. The monk who had been prescient enough to design this former monastery with benches outside each main door clearly deserved praise. It was as if he knew there would be a need for collapse after exiting from conversation with anyone inside.

"Where is Sister Paul now?" I was half afraid she would appear from behind a tree and chastise us for not immediately going to the faculty room. That image also brought Sal to mind and I wondered where he would be sent after his interview was over.

"She is sitting with Mrs. Boone. Susan Mullen will bring Laurie over once she arrives."

"I hope they let Johnny go with her," I said, a bit distractedly, feeling the menace creep back into the forefront of my mind at the thought of what Laurie would endure.

I glanced at my watch, which read 7:46. The students were required to be in homeroom by eight o'clock.

"You called some students?" I asked Ginny, thinking back to when I had seen she, the secretaries, Elizabeth Maccabe, Dolores, and Sister Paul move en masse into the Towers.

"Yes. Bernadette and her magic census program spit out a list of students by geographic location. She presumed that the students who lived the closest would be the ones we could catch at home."

Ginny's curls bounced in admiration. Bernadette had her issues and was decidedly impolite for a secretary, but she was impressively organized. Sharing similar traits, Ginny was able to overlook Bernadette's shortcomings better than some of the other teachers.

"After attendance is taken for the students in the cafeteria, their parents need to be contacted before we can dismiss them. Except for the football players."

"What do you mean?" I spoke sharply, feeling a bit protective of them.

"I guess because they practiced late last night, the detectives want to interview them. So their parents need to come down here or they have to fax over a consent form, allowing Sister Paul to sit in on the interviews."

I put my head in my hands and groaned.

"This is so complicated."

"I know. If it had happened anywhere else but a school…"

Ginny glanced at me quickly.

"Don't think I am blaming Tim Boone for dying here, I am not."

I let out a hard puff of air.

"I know that."

81

"But this is going to be a mess for the school. We got away with calling it an 'incident' this morning, because we were talking to harried parents at seven in the morning."

I interrupted her.

"But once the news reports someone was murdered on the campus of our snotty, private school…"

"So it was definitely murder?" Ginny asked, looking paler than before.

"Hell, forget I said that. And make sure you look surprised if the detectives announce it at the meeting."

"Sure," Ginny said, now distracted too.

"Sister will have to post a letter on the website, it's the fastest way to reach the parents and get the truth out." She was talking quietly, more to herself, than me.

"But part of that truth," I began, thinking back to what Detective Lawson had said.

"Is that we are a large, open campus, with hardly any security."

Ginny nodded her head. "We all thought because the kids were well behaved, that we had nothing to worry about."

"Well," she said, standing. "That is all going to change now."

We resumed our walk to the academic building, but though I was no longer shivering, the sun did not seem nearly as bright.

The noise from the collected faculty could be heard as soon as we entered the building.

"Get ready," Ginny whispered as she opened the door for me to enter.

Had the circumstances been less tragic I might have gotten some bitter amusement from the way the group froze when I entered.

Though it could have only lasted a moment, the silence allowed me to see the entire room, as though it had been frozen in time as well. Called the faculty room, this space was never meant to be a room large enough to comfortably hold the entire faculty. It was a place for teachers to go during their prep periods and lunch times, but due to the staggered nature of scheduling, no more than a third of the faculty was ever free at the same time. Some also had their own hiding places and only came here to pick up their mail.

As I scanned the room I saw how our lines were typically drawn. The men of science stood in one corner, Noah's eyes following me as I entered. Jeremy Wrobleski, in typical fashion, was standing sentinel at the window, craning his neck to see everything he could. I did not doubt he reported his findings aloud to anyone unfortunate to be near.

In one corner of the vast red couch, Toni Anne sat with Ken hovered above her. Otherwise people were grouped largely by department, though the other three members of the math department did stand the across the room from Scott. He had found a chair, despite his later arrival, and was still grading his papers, uncaring to what went on around him. I did not think the room had come to a standstill when he walked in.

Clearly the rumor mill was fully operational, even at this early hour, and everyone was aware that I had seen Tim Boone's body and reacted poorly. Knowing what that information could do, for people skilled in the art of innuendo, made me sick.

Joe Torres, as my friend, was the first to break the silence, loudly.

"How are you holding up Addra?"

I smiled at him and began to navigate my way over to his corner, with Ginny moving carefully behind me.

As soon as I reached his side, I smiled at this familiar situation. Like the men of science, Joe preferred his corners, the better to view and judge the people around him.

"I can't really say much about it," I told him, not really as a warning to him, but simply because I was afraid my emotions, now compartmentalized, would appear again for the entertainment of the crowd.

"Vultures," he said, in response.

I had already worried that my accident and the scars that attended it made me an object of attention and that now would be worse.

Someone spoke from behind us.

"We are supposed to stay here, until Sister Paul gets us."

Another person answered, I believed it was Mark though I had not actually spotted him as I walked across the room.

"At least we should get out of here early."

Someone else countered in the negative, believing that one way or another, we would be staying here all day.

I fought the urge to lash out at these people, for such grossly selfish thoughts in the face of Tim's death. The fact that Tim was murdered must be known to at least some of them and everyone had to realize that he had been the parent of one of our students. That should have been enough to quell any indifference to the event. But people did always have the ability to surprise me, despite my advancing age, and I stood there, listening to more complaints about schedule changes, missing quizzes, and hunger.

Strangely, no one even seemed to be expressing fear, as though Tim's murder was somehow removed from all of our lives, despite haven taken place right here. I found it all senseless, until I began to consider that all this talk was merely a bulwark against the heinousness of this crime. Moreland had always been a safe place and I was not the only one who had counted on that until learning otherwise.

In a way that was more customary to a cocktail party where the number of guests far outnumbered the available chairs, Ginny and Joe eventually drifted away as the various groups in the faculty room shifted. It was then that I felt undefended against Jeremy Wrobleski, who would doubtless be sidling over to me.

Somehow sensing this, or perhaps just seeing that I was alone, Noah appeared at my side. He positioned himself as a kind of shield, blocking me from the view of the room. I took the opportunity to rest my heated face against the coolness of the window.

"How are you really?"

My smile, which I placed upon my face in polite acknowledgment of his arrival, began to waver just a bit. There was something about the gentleness of his voice when asking me. It was similar but still very different from how Joe had spoken when I first entered the room.

"I just can't believe that this has happened," I said. "I cannot even bear to think about Laurie and Mrs. Boone."

"I know," he answered. "We have all had to deal with the death of our student's parents, but murder? This is new for me, no matter what Sister Paul might think of the Boston public school system."

He peered at me, with his head down, perhaps questioning how his small attempt at levity would be received.

I did smile, more for his effort than his humor.

"No, nothing like this has ever happened. I don't think I can recall any murder like this. Traffic deaths..." I paused a bit after that, but then continued.

"Some domestic incidents too, but not this. Even in Binghamton…"

I allowed my voice to trail off; confident my point had been suggested. The closest city to Moreland was Binghamton, with a population of around fifty thousand people. It proudly maintained the feel of a quintessential college town despite its size. It had its fair share of drug related crimes, but Tim's death had nothing to do with drugs.

For some reason, my brain slide a little sideways at that thought, but before I could pursue why, Sister Paul entered with Detective Lawson and another man.

"Ladies and gentlemen, the detectives had hoped to speak with you after the students were dismissed for day but that is taking a bit longer than we expected, so if you could give these detectives your attention."

Detective Lawson, made a move as if to begin speaking, but Sister was not yet done.

"After we take a moment to bow our heads in prayer."

I heard, more than saw, Jeremy Wrobleski stir, but Sister quelled his attempt to speak by leading the prayer herself.

"Heavenly Father, we come to you confused and saddened by the loss of one of our own family, Laurie Boone's father Timothy. We pray that Laurie and her mother Anne find peace in your love. And we pray, dear Lord, that we may all have the strength to lead St. Augustine's through these troubling times. Amen."

After a deep breath, Sister continued, "Now please, take a moment for your own silent prayers."

I noted Detective Lawson and his partner bowing their heads, but using their open eyes to scan the crowd. Shutting mine before I could be caught in my glance, I prayed to God to protect us all but, amongst these people, many of whom now seemed like strangers, I risked no thoughts of Tim.

With a nod to Sister Paul, Detective Lawson cleared his throat and began to speak, his resemblance to Sister heightened as they stood side by side.

"My name is Detective Lawson and this is Detective Hausler," he said, nodding to the man on his right.

"We are from the Broome County police department. We want to share some important information with you now and will be asking a few of you to speak to us privately after we are finished here."

I saw some people look about the room, visually seeking those most likely to be escorted out by the detectives. Given the direction of my own interview I anticipated they would want to speak with Toni Anne and Lucille, having no doubt also sought out Bernadette for the same reason.

"But please, it should go without saying but I am saying it anyway. Anything shared here must not be repeated to anyone. Understand the media will try to contact some of you. Once the news reports that a death occurred on this campus, your friends will start asking, and people at the supermarket, doctor's office, etc. Do not give out any specific information. If you do, you will not only be compromising the investigation but also the school."

He paused again, when Sister Paul rested a hand on his arm and spoke.

"I will have to answer some serious questions about the safety of this campus and significant alterations will have to be made. But please, that for the sake of the school and our positions in it, we must fight to keep our students."

I watched Sister carefully, pained by how old she appeared. We had all read of private schools' whose funding and support vanished, after one form of scandal or another. Sister was warning us that this scandal could cause St. Augustine's to shut its doors and all of us to lose our jobs. I did not believe she was exaggerated in this fear and hoped people like Jeremy Wrobleski understood.

The other detective, Hausler, stepped forward.

"We can tell you that Timothy Boone arrived on campus at 5:30 and entered the athletic building, perhaps with his own key, though it has not been recovered yet. This is according to Sal Vacarro, the janitor, who witnessed Mr. Boone exiting his car. After performing other duties, Mr. Vacarro returned to the athletic building at approximately 6:20, where he found Mr. Boone dead."

Hausler looked up, as if to gauge his audience.

"And he did not die by his own hand."

Here I detected a few sharply drawn breathes, but no real vocal expressions of shock, if that's what the detective was expecting. Sister and I had already warned Lawson about this school. To most of the teachers, gossip was their life's blood. Descriptions of Tim's battered body had no doubt reached the majority of them before seven o'clock.

"We have much ground to cover before we can determine if Mr. Boone's death was a random occurrence, or one specific to his life, or a crime specific to the school. The campus will remain closed to all until Wednesday."

Here there were more distinct grumblings, which earned us all a glare from Sister Paul.

Detective Lawson moved to speak again.

"If anyone can think of information relevant to this case, please do not hesitate to share it. We will be leaving our cards on this table." He threw the cards down with some emphasis, before continuing, a bit more hostility in his manner than before.

"I will need to see Lucille Bartlett and Toni Anne Tancredi."

With that, he and Detective Hausler walked out, and were quickly followed by Lucille who had the look of a person with a thing or two on their mind.

Holding up her hand, for silence, Sister spoke again.

"Please heed everything that the detectives said here. And note I will be making an announcement shortly about dismissal. We must wait until the remaining students are picked up by their parents. I will be communicating with all of you and the parents, through the website later on today. May I ask for a few volunteers to help with the students in the cafeteria and with their parent's entering the lot?"

Like the detectives before her, Sister did not wait to see if volunteers would follow her, she simply left.

From my corner I saw Ginny, Joe, and the men of science move towards the door. Noah and I did as well. Turning back to pocket a card from the detectives, I noticed Toni Ann finally getting up from her position on the couch. I could not swear to it, but I thought she and Ken were smiling.

"Ms. Lake? Are we really going home?"

"Ms. Lake, does that mean we won't have homework this weekend?"

"Ms. Lake, what about the summer reading tests? My friend told me his class got them back yesterday."

I dealt with these questions as best I could, offering what I hoped to be reassuring smiles, and gentle pushes towards the door when Noah called out a name. He was posted at the cafeteria entrance, to announce the student whose parent had lined up next at the entrance of the academic building. Once verification was made and the student released, the men of science would help guide the cars out of the lot. It was a slow process but the student population only numbered around 400 and many of those had already been told not to come to school while others had been given permission to walk home, as they usually did.

I saw that Dolores Donovan was leading some other parents down the hall to Ginny's classroom. That must be where the football players were being held, awaiting their interviews. Given what Detective Hausler had said, I surmised some questions would focus on what time the boys left and what doors were unlocked when they did.

"It really isn't fair," I said to Ginny, though the thoughts leading up to this conclusion had been unexpressed.

She raised her eyebrows at me.

"Why are they interviewing the football team? Isn't the safety of the grounds the responsibility of Coach Brown and Nick Morrison? And where are they?"

"I have no doubt they are already sequestered someone else around here, like you, Sal, and Scott Pearson were. They have the most questions to answer."

I nodded while she continued.

"They probably just want some help with a timeline from the boys. But I tell you, thank God there was a nighttime practice yesterday and nothing this morning." Ginny's shoulders shook at the possibility that students could have been present when a murder was committed. Or would their presence have prevented the murder?

I said as much to Ginny.

"I would definitely feel strange if I were Coach Brown and Nick. Ninety nine out of a hundred times they are in the building at that time but today they aren't, and this happens?" I was not sure how I would deal with

89

that, especially if I were the coach, whom I took to be a friend of Tim's. Irrational as it was, I was already feeling the stirrings of guilt in my stomach, though I was unsure why.

Ginny and I walked towards the entrance with Noah, as the last student, my new 10th grade friend, Katie was being led away by her mother. Thus far the parents had been accepting of our "incident on the campus" explanation for the cancellation of the school day. We were met by Stan Grimm, who had pushed past Katie and her mother without a glance.

"The Channel Five news truck tried to get in."

Ginny didn't bother to shush him, since Katie and her mom were already well on their way down the path. When they turned to wave back at us, Katie's hair blended with the gold color of the leaves surrounding her.

Ginny turned to me, looking more bereft than I had ever seen her.

"I wonder if they'll be back."

Chapter 6

After what seemed to be a lifetime of nightmares, I gave up trying to sleep. Stumbling into my kitchen, I wondered if Tim had risen at 4:30 yesterday. Did he stand in his quiet kitchen, waiting for the coffee to brew? Did he creep around in the dark, shoes in hand, worried about waking his family?

Trying to shake these thoughts, along with all of my others, I went about turning on every light in my home. What was it that the darkness of pre-dawn seemed even darker than that of night?

Beyond waiting for my coffee, I was not sure what to do. The nightmares had been so relentless that they had followed me into wakefulness. I felt them, like a physical force, pulling me.

The most gruesome of the dreams had brought me back to the sight of my accident. Like always, I could smell the decaying leaves, I could feel the dampness sink into my clothes. But this time, there was no car to destroy my leg, instead, it was Tim. He stood above me, already bloodied in death, and pulverized my leg with the same bar bell that had killed him. Each time he raised the weight above his head, Tim screamed, "He was already here."

Shaking free of that was going to be hard. I needed aspirin and coffee. I also knew I would need exercise. When first telling Tim about my nightmares, he had suggested physical fatigue as the best way to quell the mind and force it to rest.

Once the sun rose I would take a particularly long walk. Beyond that, I did not know what I would do. I was exceedingly mindful of Detective Lawson's warning and did not even want to risk going out to the supermarket. Luckily, at least in this respect, I lived on enough frozen and boxed food that I could skip a trip or two.

Sister Paul had also wanted the faculty gone as quickly as possible yesterday, once students were no longer in attendance. That meant leaving without revisiting our classrooms. My summer reading exams would remain incomplete and I was disappointed in myself for even being irritated by this.

I could only imagine what the rest yesterday held for Sister. Beyond having to represent some parent's for the football interviews, doubtless a long meeting with the board of directors took place. The board was a shadowy group, rarely seen, but they did technically hold Sister Paul's job in their collective hands. But should she have to answer for this? No school administrator would ever conceive of the possibility of murder within their walls. Nor would any board of directors look kindly upon the one who argued that such a possibility should be considered. Who thought of that kind of evil and expected to meet it?

Maybe Detective Lawson did, which made me feel sad for him. I stared at his business card, which lay upon my battered kitchen table. I wondered if the detectives had made any progress. What had been on Hausler's alarming list of possibilities? The murder could have been random, specific to Tim's life, or connected to the school. I wondered, given the last, how deeply the school would be investigated, and, naturally, what the police would find.

After one cup of coffee I removed myself to the bathroom, to splash cold water on my face. The caffeine in my percolated coffee was doing strange things to my heart but the rest of my body felt deadened. My eyes were gritty, the product of too many tears and too little sleep.

At 5:30, while nursing cup three, Ginny called. Having expected her too, I answered immediately, still marveling at the darkness outside.

"Are you up?" she asked unceremoniously and, of course, unnecessarily.

"Since 4:30." I responded.

"Ouch."

"I cannot believe how dark it seems," I said, apparently unable to let this observation go.

"Yeah, we are supposed to get rain later."

That made sense, I thought to myself, given the particular way my ankle and knee were aching. I had been worried when I rose, that my pain had been produced during the night. With each blow from the imaginary bar bell, my actual leg had jerked and kicked out.

"So," Ginny asked, "how are you?"

"I don't know," I responded, honestly. "Yesterday was bad. I even thought about calling Leslie."

Leslie had been the psychologist I was assigned in the hospital.

"I told you to come home with me," Ginny shrieked.

And she had, many times, while walking me to my car. I had appreciated each offer but could not have imagined accepting. My own quiet home could not save me from a colossal headache. My head would have exploded at Ginny's house.

She was loud and seemed to grow louder the further she moved from St. Augustine's. Her husband Fred was also loud. In fact he was at his loudest when yelling at their twin boys, freshman at SUNY Binghamton. Though six foot four and basketball phenoms, Jack and Joe did not have the sense God gave them, as Ginny said fondly and she made them live at home.

It went without saying that the boys were also loud. Ginny's two dogs were loud. Even her ancient cat, could, upon occasion, hiss loudly, usually when I was anywhere near. I loved Ginny's family, but conducive to peace they were not.

Once again I informed her how grateful I was for the offer, but played it off, lest another be forthcoming, as being impossible for me to sleep anywhere but my own bed. I was speaking the truth. It had taken months to perfect the pillow arrangement to compensate for my frozen calf muscles, pulled knee, and aching back.

"Why didn't you call Leslie?" Ginny asked, her voice coming and going from the phone. It sounded like she was either eating or preparing to eat while talking.

Without actually answering her question my mind began to flit over the events of yesterday morning.

"It was the perfect time," I answered her instead. "The perfect time for Tim to be murdered."

"What do you mean?" She asked sharply, perhaps thinking I had information about Tim that I had not shared with her.

"I'm sorry; I meant that it was the perfect hour. Look out your front window, I know it is Saturday, but I bet not that many people are stirring even during the week. And if they are up, they are slumped over in their kitchen, not paying attention to much else."

I was warming to my theme, and continued to speak quickly.

"The football boys weren't there. No other team was practicing. Coach Brown wasn't there. Nick Morrison was not there and he is always there."

"But Addra, you do realize what this means?" Ginny asked after a moment of consideration.

I did but wanted to hear her say it first.

"The killer has to be connected to the school. Nobody else would know that there would be no morning practice. Coach said it was a last minute decision, since the team had stayed pretty late the night before."

I didn't bother asking Ginny where she had heard that.

"I am not saying the murderer is at the school but just someone who could find out the comings and goings."

"So," I picked up, "that could be any member of a football kid's family; I guess it could be anybody around the 10th avenue cul de sac, who heard Thursday's practice and knew it meant nothing for Friday."

Ginny interjected,

"It could be Coach Brown, Nick Morrison…hell, it could even be anybody who stayed late at school of Thursday, they could have overheard Coach announce the cancellation."

I thought for a moment, but did not think that likely. I knew from the occasional complaints that

94

practice could run into the night. Not even Scott Pearson stayed that late.

"Don't forget how the kids communicate on line too. Most of them don't even bother to block their comments. You can get a good laugh out of them sometimes."

As a mother or two decidedly foolhardy sons, I could see how Ginny might peruse such outlets, but I could not help thinking it was an invasion of privacy even if the kids were not savvy enough to prevent strangers from reading their thoughts. Besides I had no desire to learn the real opinions of the students I taught.

"What about Johnny Marchiano?" Ginny asked next.

"Can you picture that? Why would he?" I asked, genuinely perplexed. Tim's wife knew about Johnny, even if we could not yet confirm that Tim did. But I could not have created a more perfect boyfriend, had I been some demented Dr. Frankenstein bent on matching deserving teens with the most appropriate mates.

"I know, I know. But the theories I am hearing are already getting crazy."

Considering the very early hour, I had to surmise that Ginny had spent the better part of yesterday on the phone. I could only hope that she had confined her speculations to other teachers at St. Augustine's and had not so quickly forgotten Sister Paul's and Detective Lawson's admonitions to silence.

"What are people saying?" I asked, almost against my own judgment.

"Joe thinks Mark did it, just to get a long weekend out of it." She snorted. I could just bear the gallows humor with equanimity, so maybe that was progress.

"Anybody saying it was me?" I asked, prepared for the answer I knew was coming.

"Yup, you were having an affair with Tim, that's why you were at school so early. And he broke it off, enraging you."

"And I beat him to death with my cane?"

Ginny snorted, "Something like that."

I looked over at my cane, which was a decidedly cheery example, festooned with daisies. These rumors were ridiculous but I did fear that they would take the police's focus from finding the real killer. I sighed.

"Did you see the website yet?"

"Ginny, I have been glued to my kitchen table since 4:30...what did Sister Rose say?"

I would read her letter myself, but had no problem with Ginny summarizing it for me now. Sister had a work ethic like Ginny's and no similar family duties to draw her away from that work. I knew the letter would be posted as early as yesterday afternoon.

"She handled it well," Ginny began. Wanting to be chair person did not preclude Ginny from also wanting to be a member of the administration and she often critiqued their actions based upon what she herself would do in the same position.

"She referenced the death and Tim's connection to the school. She also explained to the parents that she had already met with the Board of Directors and monies were going to be immediately allocated for the improvement of the security system."

I interrupted here.

"So she will improve upon Sal occasionally driving the golf cart around campus? We have no security."

"Well you and I knew that and the parents did too if they ever thought about it, but the point is, none of us ever thought about it. But Sister says there will be some suitably high tech system in place by the time classes resume on Wednesday."

"Wow," I said, the speedy finality of her pronouncement was impressive.

"There are going to be security cameras. New locks installed at the major entrance points with code entries and not keys."

"She said this in the letter?" I asked, incredulous that Sister would be so specific.

"Of course not, Elizabeth Maccabe knows the security firm doing the work. Chip Mundy, Ryan's dad,

96

owns it." Ryan was a willowy junior who despised both her own and her father's name. If Ginny had this authority I knew to trust it.

I also had the unbidden thought that Ginny's methods were not really different from Jeremy Wrobleski, it was only in her motives that they diverged. This conclusion disturbed me enough that I began to crave a walk to clear my head, and begged off the phone with promises to call her back if I grew upset.

But I had decided not to be upset at that moment, because I needed to go for my walk and focus only on my steps and the cars around me. To this end, I exited my house and moved with purpose in the opposite direction of 10th street and the school.

After about forty minutes of brisk walking, which included walking up and down every block in my path, I found myself over in the more commercial side of town. This meant I was a mere block away from Tim's office, which was closed weekends.

Knowing that it was closed made me feel safe enough to walk past. But I grew suspicious when I saw a light snap on through the window. Glancing at the lot I saw one car, Audrey's silver Jeep. Feeling that I needed to say something to her, I checked the side door. It was open, but the elevator was not functioning.

I could only pray that that sounds of my clunking up the stairs did not frighten her before I reached their third floor office.

"Audrey?" I called, not wanting to try the doorknob. I could easily imagine a horror film beginning that way, especially in the office of a man just murdered in grisly fashion.

I saw the top of Audrey's bouffant bun through the glass pane, but not the eyes of the tiny girl. At least she had locked the door.

"It's Addra Lake. I was walking by and wanted to see how you are holding up."

Actually while that was true, I was also curious why she would be in the office at all the morning after Tim's death.

97

"Addra, hi." She sniffled at me but did not expect a hug, which was fine with me, being an awkward hugger, at best.

"The police are coming to get Tim's patient files, and I am trying to separate out the current ones."

"They can do that?" I asked. I realized that Tim was not a doctor but I was still a bit perturbed by this apparent breach in confidentiality.

"These are just payment files, nothing about treatment. They also want the sign in books for the last six months, for some reason."

I imagined they wanted to cross reference both, to ensure that Audrey had provided them with the complete records. Did that mean that she was a suspect? I had to doubt it, Audrey was barely ninety pounds.

"The police spoke to you? Me too." I added, so that she did not think I was prying information from her, while sharing none of my own.

For a moment she seemed confused, but then her expression cleared.

"At the school, right?"

I nodded. "A Detective Lawson."

"Yeah, me too." She said.

"He came here, because I open the office. I can't believe it." She began to cry quietly, instantly taking up a tissue from one of the boxes placed at intervals throughout the room.

"I kept saying that everybody loved Tim, all his patients did, right?"

"Absolutely." I agreed, though I had no way of really knowing if that were true.

"I guess police are obsessed with money because they kept asking about it. But there is no way they will understand our billing system with insurance companies."

I peered at her, thinking.

"They asked about that?"

"I guess, but they were also talking about Tim and money. Did I think he spent within his means? Did I think he spent a lot on his wife?"

I also supposed, like money, the spouse was a common focus in any murder and I tried to not read too much into these lines of inquiry.

"It might have been my fault anyway," Audrey continued.

"How so?"

"Well, the detective guy asked me how I thought Tim and Mrs. Boone got along. I said I really didn't hear too much from her, except this one fight they had a few weeks ago. I wasn't eavesdropping," she said quickly.

"I know that, Audrey," I said in a tone that I hoped would suggest how silly she was to think otherwise.

Audrey barely listened to anything and besides, Tim's office was really just an alcove in the reception area. Anyone would be privy to a conversation he had while sitting at his desk.

"Tim just kept saying, 'Don't worry about the money, Annie. Don't worry about the money.' Do you think I got Mrs. Boone in trouble?"

"No, married people fight about money all the time. It's the most common argument." I reassured her. I had read something to that effect in a magazine though I had no idea why I recalled it, given my unmarried state.

"Yeah, and anyway, Tim didn't really ever talk about money, not in that way."

"What way?"

"About what he bought or didn't buy or coupons or stuff, like my mother."

"Ah," I said, vaguely, wondering if I shouldn't be going. I now knew why Audrey was here on a Saturday morning, and I was growing a bit concerned about that folder on her desk. She had said the police were going to come get it, didn't she? Though I felt steadier now, I did not relish seeing Detective Lawson at this moment.

"He was funny about money in other ways."

I raised my eyebrows.

"I don't know," Audrey shrugged. "Tim was just really polite I guess and acted interested in people's business and stuff, asking questions I could not be bothered to ask."

A little whisper of an idea floated into my brain, so I asked her to explain more.

"You know Mr. and Mrs. Woodley? Mr. Woodley comes here for his neck? Well, when Mrs. Woodley would sit in here, Tim was always asking her questions about their postal shipping business. Who came in? What did they ship? What was their profit margin?"

She made a face as she asked that last question.

"Tim was into profit margins."

I thought for a moment, but could not verify her impressions. Tim and I had only talked about money briefly. Or, to be truthful, he listened when I complained about the disability insurance industry and the inflated pricing of medical tests and the like. Tim had never inquired about my profit margins, but he already knew I was a private school teacher, and perhaps did not wish to embarrass me.

"Did you notice he talked to a lot of people about that stuff?"

"Yeah, I guess, when I was paying attention. But you have to remember, I have to set up all the patients, and Tim always closes the door when someone is in the back room."

I enjoyed the back room, which was a small room with two patient beds. Audrey was right, despite bordering the main patient area, where the beds were separated by curtains; it was difficult to hear once the door to the back room was closed.

"Well," I shrugged, unsure of how to end this conversation, "I would not worry about what you told the detectives. I think they only ask questions they already know the answers too."

Audrey gave a small smile.

"Yeah, the detective guy already seemed to know about Dougie."

"Dougie?" I didn't think I had met a Dougie at therapy.

"Doug Dixon, the town cop who comes here for his knee? I mentioned him when the detective asked about which patients Tim seemed closest too. I mentioned you too."

I tried not to be sidetracked by that statement, however much my heart hurt to hear it. Doug Dixon was Angry Cop. Unsurprisingly his name had never come up in our dealings.

"Ang---Dougie was close to Larry?" I wasn't sure I had picked up on that.

"Sure, they were always whispering, and once I heard them talk about meeting."

When she said the word meeting, I noticed her eyes drift to the large clock above my head. I imagined the police would be getting here soon.

"I have some phone calls to make but I am glad you stopped by, to save me one. Mrs. Boone called me last night and said that her sister's were already arranging a memorial service for Tim, his...his body isn't available yet, but they want to have their closure now. That is what she said, 'closure.' So there is going to be a memorial service at St. Sebastian's Monday morning, at 10 o'clock. She wanted to make sure his patients knew."

"That is lovely," I said, "thank you."

Inside I was not thinking this service was lovely, I was thinking it was quick. Still I could see the wisdom, given the notoriety his murder will likely produce, of having a service for him now. I hoped that a private, Catholic burial would follow.

"I will see you there?" I asked, turning to go. The elevator was no doubt still off and I did not want to encounter anyone in the stairwell.

"Yup, see you there."Audrey said, her more cheery tone likely attributable to her training in reception.

Naturally I had only made the turn in the second floor stairwell when I heard footfalls below me. It stood to reason, given my track record with poor luck and worse timing, that I would meet Detective Lawson.

"Ms. Lake. You're here."

Seeing as we were picking up where we had last left off, with my feeling the need to answer his 'non-question' questions with verbiage, I took a deep breath.

"Yes. I was out for my morning walk and I saw a light on in Tim's office and went in to speak to Audrey."

"You knew she was here because of her car."

"Yes. I wanted to know about if and when therapy would be resuming."

The stairwell was too dark for me to tell by the detective's face if he thought he saw sincerity in mine.

That would have been a fine question to ask Audrey, albeit a cold hearted one, if I had thought of it.

"And what did she say?"

"She wasn't sure."

I had to pray I sounded convincing enough that he would not attempt to verify any of this with Audrey.

"I am glad I ran into you here, at Mr. Boone's office." Detective Lawson said as I recalled that this was not the first time he had mocked my phrasing of an answer about Tim. Since there was nothing I was prepared to do about that, I simply lifted my brows in inquiry.

"You know Coach Brown?" he asked.

"Yes, I suppose," I responded, not sure where we were headed.

"You suppose you know him?"

Detective Lawson was proving to be decidedly literal this morning.

"Yes, I know him. We have chatted a few times, here more than at school. I go to the football games, when I can. He has arranged some members of the team to help me carry my bags," I waggled my cane at him, lest he had forgotten.

"But I have no idea what his first name is, nor anything else about him. Oh, wait. He is taking the varsity boys to Florida Columbus Day weekend."

"Really? How is that being funded?"

"I have no idea, Detective. I assume by the parents?"

But without having to repeat that silly ditty about assumptions, I reminded myself that I had no idea how money was collected and distributed in the athletic department.

"His first name is Mike."

Detective Lawson moved passed me up the stairs. I stood, barely detecting his small smile in the dimness.

Staying focused during the walk home proved difficult but I managed. A black Ford truck turned in front of me at the Main Street traffic light and I shouted things that did not reflect well on me as a Catholic school teacher, however alliterative my comments were.

After eating a grilled cheese sandwich for lunch, I turned on my computer to read Sister Paul's letter for myself. There was also an email from her, sent en masse to everyone in the St. Augustine's directory. It announced the same memorial service that Audrey had told me about. Sister expected Laurie's homeroom, her soccer team, and the football team to attend. Naturally the same was expected of the faculty.

Shaking my head in grim anticipation of this, I noticed an email from Noah. It was terse enough to be intriguing. Citing his lack of my phone number, he simply provided his own and asked me to call him.

Not even bothering to wonder how I could be smiling, with so much wrong, I got up to retrieve my cordless telephone. Only then did I notice the message light blinking.

"Addra, this is Dolores. Would you mind dropping off the folder I lent you when school resumes Wednesday? I have determined that it is no longer necessary to pursue the matter, given all that has happened."

I had, it seemed, learned the issue which had prompted Noah to contact me. He surely received the same, expertly vague, message. It was truly masterful in how little it would reveal to an uninformed listener. The only specifics she had spoken were her own name and a day of the week.

What was going on?

I dialed the number that Noah had given me, grateful it was he who picked up the phone.

"What is going on?" I asked, with no preamble beyond identifying myself.

I could practically hear him pushing his glasses back.

"I have no idea."

"But you agree something is rotten in the state of Denmark?"

He laughed in confirmation.

"Addra, would you like to do something tomorrow? I mean, would you like to meet somewhere and talk about this, maybe at the coffee house on Main?"

"Getting too paranoid to talk over the phone?" I asked, a bit teasingly. But after I said it, paranoid was exactly how I began to feel and immediately squinted, to make sure that my front door was locked.

"Maybe." He waited a moment or two. "But, how about it?"

I calculated the likelihood of running into students or other faculty based upon the time I would suggest to him.

"Would it be alright to meet early? I can walk over there after 8:30 mass. Say, about ten after nine?"

"Great," Noah answered, sounding like he really meant it.

"Are you going to be ok today?"

I thought for a moment before answering him.

"I will be but you won't be able to say the same about my electric bill."

After he inquired I explained my plan to while away the hours watching a marathon of my patented 'feel good' movies. I did not tell him that I would also be leaving every light blazing as soon as darkness fell.

Chapter Seven

One of the practical benefits of early mass on Sunday was that, in the quiet of a mostly empty church, I felt no distractions pull on my attention. On this Sunday, I had more distractions than usual, but left them aside when I entered St. Sebastian's.

I would be returning here tomorrow to say a public farewell to Tim, but wanted to use mass today to say my own. Tim and I had not been typical friends and our relationship was, in a peculiar way, consumer based. But he had been just the right type of person to help me in my recovery. I did not find comfort in other people easily, but found it with Tim. I wanted to take today to thank him for that, in a way that I hoped he would hear.

After mass was over I was still heavy of heart, but felt better than I had before. Father Jensen had said mass as he usually did, at warp speed, and I noted I still had twenty minutes before I was to meet Noah. A walk would help my stiff muscles, but I was worried about the effect of the fresh air on my carefully applied makeup. Each time I saw Noah I was, in one way or another, not at my best. I could not deny taking a bit more time with my preparations this morning, and did not want to see the effort wasted on a phalanx of busy squirrels.

I resolved then to walk slowly, trying to keep my hair from taking any sort of unnecessary flight. There was nothing I could do about the makeup, having not yet solved the mystery of why it disappeared within an hour of my leaving the house.

Once again schooling myself to focus on nothing but the walk ahead of me and the cars around, I went left from church, down a side street that ran parallel to Main. There were several points where I could go back, and would not be late for my coffee date. I decided to call it a date and see how I felt about that, aware that I would feel better if Noah had called it one first.

I had only just turned on Belfast Road when I became aware of a car riding in the street behind me. This street, near to St. Sebastian's grammar school, did have speed bumps, and I imagined the driver was being cautious because of them. I always applauded careful driving and turned to give a smile, if not actual applause.

It was not however, a car in the road, but a truck, and one that had its windows tinted. It was still motoring behind me, with no apparent inclination to pass. I was suddenly uncomfortable and tried to think of what I should do. My brain was sluggish after a second night of too little sleep. It only seemed able to recall a fact I had heard once, that many women are attacked because they are too embarrassed to call out for help.

I was gearing myself up to scream like a banshee when the passenger window rolled down, and Coach Brown called to me from the driver's seat.

"Hey, Addra, I was not sure that was you."

I closed my mouth and glared at him. We were in our small town, with me at 5'9, with gigantic hair, and a cane emblazoned with yellow daisies. He knew full well it was me, but had he tried to scare me?

Remembering what Detective Lawson had told me yesterday, I shouted,

"Hi, Mike, do you want to pull over?" If I was going to have to speak to him, I would neither step into the street nor scream over the roar of his augmented engine. I would also not be getting into his truck, but merely leaning against the same open passenger window.

"What are you up to?" He asked, as though we had just encountered each other casually.

"Well, for the last five minutes, I was wondering why a truck was following me."

He laughed at that, even though I was not trying to be funny.

"What are you really doing?" He asked again.

"I just left church. What are you doing?" I did not really care but if he was intent on knowing my plans I would demand to know his.

"Those detectives have called me back to their house, on a Sunday."

He squeezed the steering wheel in apparent anger, an emotion which sat upon the coach's countenance strangely. I had always seen him as a distinctively affable man, who never seemed unduly emotional, even from the sideline of his own games.

"Ah," I said, for lack of anything better. Considering what Detective Lawson had asked me in the stairwell of an empty building, I assumed he had Mike Brown in his sights.

"How many times have they interviewed you?"

"Twice," I answered, with a backward glance towards the church. I had technically spoken to Detective Lawson twice, and decided to count our conversation in the stairwell as an interview, impromptu though it was.

"Yeah, well, this is my third one and they keep bothering my kids. Asking about my keys and if I give them out, and how many times I lose them. Sister Paul has been asking me the same thing."

He looked at me like I was to agree these questions were absurd and not salient, as I actually found them. If Coach Brown was lending out his keys to students, or 'losing' them a lot, then the safety of the kids was being compromised. My mind floated back to the cigarette strewn alley, where I saw those tire marks. How well did Coach really watch 'his kids?'

"What did they ask you, Addra?"

"I guess what you would expect. How well I knew Tim, what his connection to the school was."

Coach Brown interrupted me.

"Did that detective ask about me?"

"Yes," I answered immediately and honestly. What did the coach expect?

"Coach, Tim was on campus at your invitation and died in the football weight room. It is only logical," I was cut off again, which was making this conversation even more tedious.

"Yeah, but I am hardly the only one at school that Tim was 'involved with.'"

Coach used that hand gesture, meant to suggest quotation marks, when he noted Tim's involvement with people other than himself. What was he implying? Before

I could marshal the nerve to ask him, he went on, talking more to himself than to me.

"Those detectives want to know about the Florida trip, why?"

Here I grimaced a bit, wondering if I had been the one to direct their attention southward.

"I'm taking care of that trip, it has nothing to do with the school. The football parents are generous, so what?"

Coach Brown looked in my general direction, but obviously this was not a conversation of give and take. My arm was growing numb, leaning against his truck, and I wanted to see Noah.

"Everybody horse trades at that school, believe me."

I turned again to look back at the church. I wanted to get away from the coach, but I also felt like I could glean from him some vital pieces of information about St. Augustine's. What they had to do with Tim's murder, I did not know.

"Nick warned me about that snake." The coach muttered.

"Tim?" I asked, trying to keep some track of this disjointed conversation.

"Him? Yeah, he was a snake but I am talking about Jeremy Wrobleski. Can you imagine how many times he has called those detectives already?"

I could easily imagine him pocketing all the remaining cards that Detective Lawson had left in the faculty room but again did not see how this was relevant to Tim's murder. If we were discussing Wrobleski's death, it would be another story, though I felt a bit guilty to think that.

"What do you think Jeremy could have said?"

Instead of answering Coach Brown put his car back into gear.

"I need to get going. See you tomorrow."

I was given about a nanosecond to back up before the coach roared away from the curb, without signaling. I squinted to see his license plate as he sped up the street.

My watch revealed that I was now going to be late, so I turned back towards Main Street, shaking my head the entire time.

The coffee shop, called The Big Bean, distinguished itself from its competition by the multi colored bean bags dotting the light wood floor. I fell into that large demographic however that could not get up from a bean bag chair, once I managed to get into one. For us, traditional tables and chairs lined the far wall. Noah sat at one of these tables and turned towards the door when the chimes announced my arrival.

I would rather he not watch me walk across the room but could hardly stop him.

"I waited to order," he said, by way of greeting. He seemed rather jittery already and I wondered if coffee was not a poor choice for his beverage.

"Ok," I said, hanging my cane on the back of my chair. Walking with a cane in one hand and a purse dangling from the opposite shoulder had long ago grown tiresome. I now managed with my cell phone, keys, and small wallet tucked into various pockets. Having spent most of my adulthood with cavernous purses I did find this liberating, despite never having a tissue when I needed one.

"Sorry," Noah said to his folded hands. "Sorry. I guess I'm nervous."

He glanced up in time to see my quizzical expression. Why was he nervous? Did he believe Dolores would follow us here? Was he worried I, as one of the gossiped about murderers, would kill him after crumb buns?

Dismissing those, I also looked at his folded hands while I asked,

"Is this a date?"

I then watched his hand move to squeeze mine, while he answered, "yes."

"Hey Addra." Two menus now appeared next to our tangled hands. I figured one of us had better look up.

"How are you, Brian?"

This was Brian, of the underdeveloped calf muscles, who I assumed knew of Tim's demise.

"Man, this is crazy about Tim. Audrey called me about the service tomorrow. I am working a double shift today so I can go."

"That's great, hon. I am glad she reached you. Brian, this is my friend Noah. He works at the school as well."

"Hey, man, cool." Brian answered."Let me get your coffees."

I wondered briefly what he thought was cool while he retrieved his pen.

"Addra, the usual? Noah?"

To my dismay, Noah ordered a plain, black coffee. When I meet Brian's eyes I gave a small nod. He might wonder if I should change my order, seeing how spartan Noah's meal would be, but I was old enough to embrace the sugar loving side of myself without shame.

Noah gave me a wide smile, after Brian drifted away.

"So," he asked, "what is the usual?"

"Do you miss anything?" I was smiling myself.

"Not when I am paying attention."

"Well," I began, wanting to tell him about my peculiar encounter with Mike Brown.

"I was paying attention on my way but I have no idea why Coach Brown grabbed me for a chat."

Noah brow furrowed from behind his glasses.

"Just now?"

"Yes. A truck was following me up Belfast Avenue and when I turned to confront it, Coach rolled down his window and wanted to talk. He was on his way to his third police interview."

"And…" Noah waved me on, looking a bit tense.

"I'm not sure. He seemed pretty manic, half angry and half afraid. He wasn't really talking to me, exactly."

I got my elbows off the table a second before Brian sloshed my drink down. With it, came the plate bearing my two maple crullers. This was my usual, with or without a guest.

"What is that?" Noah nodded towards my colossal, whipped cream topped concoction.

"This," I said with awe, "is the Triple Chocolate Threat. Brian is a genius at making them." I raised my cup to toast Brian, who was watching for my reaction. I sipped and sighed with delight.

"What did Brown say?"

Noah was drinking his coffee with nothing added to it. I attempted to process that fact while also recounting what Coach Brown had said.

"He seemed to feel that the police were unfairly focusing on him and what I gathered was his habitually sloppy care with his keys and locking up."

I thought for a minute, and absently broke off pieces of my glazed donut.

"Then he kept making these strange declarations that he would never really follow up on. He said Jeremy Wrobleski was a snake and he thinks Jeremy told the detectives that he gets things from the parent's of his players."

Noah's eyes narrowed. "What do you mean?"

"Again, I am not totally sure, but Coach said a lot of people horse-trade at the school and he is not the only one. I guess some parents are willing to sponsor a lot of purchases to guarantee their son plays. He also said he was not the only one who was involved with Tim. But he did not specifically connect these two facts together nor did he say what qualified as involvement with Tim."

"And then," Noah began, while finally reaching to take a bite of a cruller before I devoured both of them.

"There is the issue of Boone's daughter's poor grades and her acceptance into the Honors Program."

"Which Coach Brown could have been intimating she got because of a deal that Tim Boone made with someone at the school?"

"But what kind of deal could he have made?" I was confused and beginning to feel a deep pain in my heart over all the secrets that apparently surrounded me.

"And who are the people in the school making these unethical deals? Not Dolores."

I looked across at Noah.

"You're thinking that she would not have turned us on to this problem if she was the one who created it? But if she were trying to distance herself from the discovery, that must mean she knows or suspects who pushed these students through."

"But who could do that?"

I thought for a long moment.

"Sister Paul, of course, though I cannot imagine she would. Nick Morrison must have some pull, as Athletic Director, but over the Honor's Program..."

"What about the secretaries?" Noah asked me. "In my experience they are the ones who actually handle the paperwork and really know what is going on."

I thought back to Bernadette and her 'magic' with the school census program.

"Have you met Bernadette and Janine?" I asked him. Our school ran quite effectively with these two women sharing the duties, though nominally, Bernadette worked for Sister Paul, and Janine for Dolores Donovan.

"I did, briefly, while I was waiting for my interview. Janine is the normal one?"

I gave a particularly unladylike snort. Noah had asked the most effective question to explain Bernadette by.

"Bernadette went to Tim for physical therapy." I told him.

"But what could she have been trading Tim for?"

Brian came by with a refill for Noah, at the same moment he was asking that last question.

"Tim was into a lot." He said, giving us another hint of a perspective I had evidently not known.

"What do you mean, Brian? I am starting to think I really missed a lot of what went on at therapy."

"He could make a deal, that's all. Got Dougie to get him these diet pills that cost an arm and a leg."

"Tim was on a diet?" I found that hard to believe.

"Nah, but his wife needed those pills, bad. Dougie and Tim were always whispering about something."

I thought back to my own experience with their secretive conversations, not long before Tim had been murdered, as well as the conversation I overhead between Angry Cop and Audrey. Brian's information made their meaning clearer.

"It was weird though, because Dougie always talked to me about how much he hated Tim. But then there they were, whispering all the time."

Shrugging off the hypocrisy of his elders, Brian slapped down our check.

"Why are you frowning?" Noah asked me as Brian left.

"Dougie is a local police officer I call 'Angry Cop" and I am not comfortable with the idea that he was 'getting' Tim pills."

"And?"

"And Brian said Angry Cop hated Tim. That is the first time I have heard an emotion like hate connected to Tim, though I guess Coach Brown did say he was a snake too."

Noah reached for the check.

"I suppose Jeremy won't be the only person calling the detectives."

There was not even a hint that Noah was being snide, but I was troubled by his comment anyhow.

"I am not a busy body or a snoop," I said, rather sharply.

"I know that. You need this solved."

Noah was right. Of course any right minded citizen of this town wanted Tim's murderer caught. All members of the St. Augustine community wanted Laurie to find peace and the school to return to safety. But I did need this solved, for less clear reasons.

I still felt menace all around me, which was growing stronger the more I learned that nothing I counted on was as it appeared to be.

"I love St. Augustine's." I said, knowing that Noah would understand.

113

He looked at me with sad eyes, perhaps divining that all the secrets around me, once found out, could destroy that feeling.

After settling into Noah's ancient and comfy car, I gave him directions to my house. Moreland was not so big that these directions needed to be repeated. It felt strange to be here, with him, knowing that we both considered this the conclusion of our first date, but spent all of it on the subjects of murder and deception.

Without being asked, Noah pulled into my driveway, so I could reach my house more easily.

"This is nice," he said, meaning my small, Cape style home. "I rent."

"Years ago, when my parents moved to Florida, they gave me, what they called my inheritance. My dad said they planned on going to Florida to squander their money any way they saw fit, so he wanted me to have some while I could."

I was grinning when I said this, but mostly because I knew my dad was serious. Daddy was always serious about how devoutly he avoided serious things.

"So I bought the house while I was still in graduate school."

"You've always lived alone?" Noah asked.

"Yes, but only sometimes have I lived lonely." I looked at him with the same question.

"I lived with someone in Boston. We were together a long time without getting married until she came home one day wanting to marry someone else."

"I'm sorry." I said at the same time he was shaking his head.

"If I really wanted to marry her I would have. We were just together because of inertia."

I wanted to tell him that I understood what he meant, that I often worried that most of my life could be explained through the force of the same.

But I didn't say anything and grew still when Noah turned and reached his arm towards me.

Rummaging in the back seat for a moment, he came up with Dolores's file.

114

"I think she believes you were holding on to this."

"Ah, yes." I said.

"I'll just toss this in my car for now. And I have to gather up the gumption to call Detective Lawson."

"I am driving Stan Grimm to the service tomorrow."

As far as goodbyes went, this one lacked romance.

I made sure my keys were in my hand and then got out of the car, holding on to Dolores' folder carefully. She would certainly want to know why it appeared to have gone through the wash cycle already and I didn't want to make it any more bedraggled. After depositing it in my trunk, I made my way up to my doorway.

When my doorbell rung a moment after locking it, I must admit I was annoyed. Then Noah reached for me and we kissed until I was breathless.

Walking down St. Sebastian's center aisle with Ginny, I allowed my eyes to scan the church, struck by how different it looked today. What had been comforting yesterday now seemed foreboding and cold. The church was also dark, the high lights doing little to dispel the gloom of the sunless day.

Most mourners wore dark colors but did not seem to adhere to the formal dress code I had been taught was proper for church. As Ginny and I sought our seats I heard the distinct squeak of someone doing the same in sneakers. Ginny lead the way to the rows of St. Augustine students and teachers. Like at a school sponsored mass, teachers sat on the aisle seats, to provide students with a constant reminder of how to behave. I did not think their behavior would be an issue today; the ones here were here for Laurie.

My eyes found her and her mother in the front row, beside a large framed photograph of Tim. Laurie did not wear her black suit well. I recalled how, in the summer, she only wore pink, a choice which matched her sweet disposition. Today her clothes looked alien on her, which I supposed befitted this foreign experience. She looked lost too, even with her mother on one side and Johnny, her boyfriend, on the other.

I focused on Anne Boone, whom I had only heard spoken of. She sat next to four other women, all bearing a striking resemblance to each other. These must be the sisters that Audrey had mentioned. They were all substantial women who bore matching solemn expressions.

Ginny nudged me.

"Don't they look pissed?"

I looked again at Mrs. Boone and her sisters. It was possible that what I took for solemnity was anger. I could not even imagine how Mrs. Boone must feel towards her husband's killer but was it also possible that she was angry at him for being murdered? I had no idea.

Turning slightly, I spared a glance across the aisle. Many of Tim's other patients were sitting together and I wondered if I should not have done the same. Brian caught my eye, sitting next to Audrey. Angry Cop, whose moniker I refused to abandon despite knowing his real name, was staring at a particularly pretty friend of Laurie's. I openly glared at him, almost completely turned around in my seat, but his lecherous look precluded noticing anything else. I was gratified to see Detective Lawson, a few rows back, follow my line of sight and frown.

I allowed myself a small smile of victory when I turned back around. But a change in the music signaled that the service was about to begin. I suddenly felt lightheaded and strangely far away.

The music gave way to readings and a eulogy by a business colleague of Tim's. The entire service was decorous and antiseptic. It was as if the manner of Tim's death was so shocking that the banality of his farewell was necessary for contrast.

It certainly helped to keep me stoic and I felt little guilt letting my mind wander. Since I did not see Noah I wondered where he and Stan sat. Knowing Detective Lawson was here made me consider the message I had left for him yesterday. Somewhat thankful he had not picked up the phone, I had laid out what I hoped was a clear recitation of all I had learned in my conversations with Audrey, Brian, and Coach Brown.

When put forth in a single streaming message, which I bookended with apologies, it might appear as though I was conducting interviews myself for some ad hoc investigation. But I was not too troubled by what the detective might think of me, provided I was not regarded as a suspect. I was more concerned over how little I seemed to know about the people around me.

It was becoming clear that what I thought of Tim did not match the person that he may have been. I could accept this, admitting that my relationship with his was extremely limited. But what of the people at St. Augustine's, whom I had known for years?

Mark had checked his watch at least six times since the service began, and he did not manage to be subtle once. Two of the men of science were playing computer games on their cell phones. Ginny had kept up a stream of sardonic commentary throughout the hour.

I knew how large her heart was and did not take her wit to be any more than that, but still I was bothered. I was also bothered by the fact that, a year ago, I would have been chuckling along with her.

When the service was completed, Mrs. Boone and Laurie only greeted a few mourners before getting into a car that pulled up to meet them. I expected this had a lot to do with the news channel van which had parked across Main Street.

"That could not have been more strange," Ginny declared as we made our way down the church steps. I agreed, but silently.

"What are you doing tomorrow?"

"I guess I will try to catch up on some work and adjust my lesson plans." I said.

"I'm going to tackle the back room," Ginny said with finality.

Her back room had once been the first floor bedroom of her father in law. Since his passing it had become the depository for all the things the Ferguson family no longer needed, only needed sometimes, or just could not bear to throw away. Ginny made a biannual pledge to bring some order to it but it remained the one spot of chaos in her otherwise organized life.

We stood for a moment, watching Mark run to his car, before making the motions that it was time to go. I never saw Sister Paul, Detective Lawson, or Noah and felt curiously fine with that. I had too much to think about.

"I'm going to walk," I told Ginny.

"Sure, sweetie. Don't worry, Wednesday will be better." She smiled at me and moved over to another group of teachers.

Expecting that Tim would still be dead on Wednesday and St. Augustine's would still be the site of his untimely murder, I lacked Ginny's confidence. I also lacked the patience to look more than once at Jeremy Wrobleski, who was conducting a conversation with the Dean, Susan Mullen, while openly staring at the news van.

Wanting nothing more to do with my fellow teachers I turned in the opposite direction towards the collection of football and soccer players. Nick Morrison was standing guard over them, but I could get away just with smiling at him. The wide shoulders of the football linemen, straining against their suits, provided excellent cover for my getaway.

My walk home would be made only slightly longer by this route. I would walk a bit further up Main until I reached a cross street that would lead back east. One deep breath cleared my mind so that I could focus on the walk and the cars that inevitably attended it. This made it easy to spot Wanda and Mitch Doyle, sitting in the window booth of Marvin's Diner.

I was immediately struck my how companionable they were together and how lucky to still enjoy each other's company so many decades into their union. As I opened the heavy diner door to join them my mind briefly skidded over thoughts of Noah and our kiss, which I had resolved to not think of while at St. Sebastian's.

"You'll eat something." Wanda stated, craning her neck to spot the waitress. I had not yet sat down, which was another reason to be fond of Wanda.

"Oh no," I said, with admirably sincere sounding conviction. "You're done already."

In truth I could not wait for the waitress to arrive. I was besotted with diner breakfasts. Eggs, bacon, and peppery home fries could only be properly prepared on the greasy grill of a diner kitchen.

"Please," Mitch said. "We'll be here all morning. They brew extra pots of coffee just for us."

I smiled, feeling instantly at ease. That was the thing about Mitch and Wanda, a few minutes spent in their company and they felt like your favorite aunt and uncle. I never thought about how I looked in front of them, never worried that my words being measured or my posture being criticized.

Margaret, the waitress who called me and everyone else doll, took my order in two seconds since I have a usual here too.

"So, how was it?" Wanda asked.

"Impersonal," I answered.

"And fast," she countered, relieving me of the need to say the same.

"Helps people forget," Mitch said, with the air of someone who has repeated this thought more than once.

"But it just happened."

"To you and the people who knew him, it just happened. To everyone else in this town, three days is a long time for a murderer to not be caught. The police are probably thrilled the wife did this so fast. No more news to report takes the pressure off them for a while."

I just mumbled that I tried to stay away from the news, which might have led me to a slightly less cynical nature than Mitch's. I appreciated what he said nevertheless.

119

"There was a blurb about your school too. It sounds like that place will be locked up tighter than Fort Knox on Wednesday."

"But what can they do about the alley?" Wanda wondered.

I kept returning to her question during my meal, even as we began to talk of other things. I didn't need to mention Mr. Delgado, because they had already learned about his camera.

"He's a fruitcake, but if he solves that particular problem I will invite him over for Christmas dinner," was Mitch's pronouncement on the subject.

"Are you walking at your usual time tomorrow, honey?"

I had to wipe my cheek before answering Wanda, as errant globs of ketchup had a way of settling there.

"I am. I plan on pretending tomorrow is like a regular school day and get a lot accomplished."

"Good, because it really throws us off when we don't see our regulars." Mitch interjected.

"It's true. We only saw the old man on Friday."

Knowing what I had been doing instead, I remained silent.

"The old man comes by when it is still dark out. That's how I know to put the coffee on."

Mitch interrupted his wife and continued.

"When you are by, at seven we know it is time for toast."

"Yes," Wanda laughed. "By 7:15 we were starving and couldn't remember why."

Chapter Eight

If any joy were to be found in my unaccustomed Tuesday home it would be in the fair amount of school work I accomplished. Some teachers, like Mark, planned their lessons and tests once at the start of their careers, and continued to use them regularly, no matter how many years passed.

I could never be comfortable doing that, and amended my plans yearly. I could hardly blame the kids for groaning over the unfamiliar language of centuries past, if I did not work to show them the relevancy of the ideas contained within. Shakespeare made this easier of course and *Hamlet*, as I had begun with the senior Honors class, even more so.

The abrupt ending to the school week had left me without any homework or exams to grade and so I was free to concentrate on my schedule for the semester. But my contentment in my work was tempered, not just by Tim's death, but by the specter of tomorrows return. I simply did not wish to go.

So much of my morning ritual, my literal path, was now sullied. So much darkness lurked on this campus and I was feeling the added burden of my failed perceptions to realize this earlier.

But duty called and my routine, come Wednesday morning, almost exactly mimicked that of Friday. I still needed to get to school early, enter my summer reading grades, and organize my tests and journals. I once again decided to forego my walk and drive to school. The crisp weather demanded I wear a coat, but I did reach for a new one, feeling both foolish and satisfied when I did so.

One notable difference in the days however, was the presence of Noah's station wagon in my driveway. Proving the insidious power of fear, I approached his car carefully and with my cell phone in my hand.

"The Bean doesn't open until seven," he said by way of introduction. I wondered if this was a habit of his, to initiate conversations with me using statements best left to the middle of the dialogue.

"I could have told you that." I answered, confused.

"You could have, if you had called. I realized too late that I did not have your phone number."

"Ah. And if I had called you?"

Noah got out of his car and reached for my school bag.

"I would have told you I was driving you to work today, to make sure it was a new kind of day."

I could not help but smile. He was reading my mind again. Walking around to the passenger side Noah helped me in and closed the door behind me. It was like my first date in high school, if my date had actually been that chivalrous.

"So the Bean doesn't open until seven," I reminded him, hoping to get the mystery of that declaration solved.

"So I brought you coffee from my house. I even put some chocolate syrup in it."

Here I laughed and accepted the travelers mug. The word 'nerd' was emblazoned on the side of it in bright red letters.

"Is this alright?" He asked.

"Well, neither one of us are married." I said a bit too quickly.

Noah kept his eyes on the road, but a question still seemed to emanate from him.

"Um, skip that."

"I like it that you don't want to gossip for gossips sake. It's hard not to feel like half the people at St. Augustine's are fishing for something every time they ask you a question."

"Hmmm," I was enjoying my syrupy coffee, though it packed an interesting punch.

"What do you think it will be like when we arrive, swat teams and search lights?"

"I have no idea, but I wonder if it won't be a case of shutting the barn door after the cow gets out. Do you suppose anyone really thinks Tim's murder was a random occurrence?"

"Beat's me, but…" Noah trailed off as we turning into the campus from Mayflower Road. Sal Vacarro was sitting in a lawn chair, beside the enormous gate that now blocked the entrance to the grounds.

"Good morning Mr. Stabler, Addra." Sal said as he lumbered up to Noah's window.

"There is a swipe key in each faculty mailbox, that you will just use like so."

He moved to swipe a flat plastic card in the small box attached to a sunken concrete pole. With swift and quiet motion, the gate opened. Thinking of how pitifully off target I could be at teller windows and toll booths, I knew I would be getting out of my car every morning, to swipe.

Sal walked back over to the window.

"I have the academic building main door opened now, because people need to get their key swipes first, but otherwise, you will have to use it and the special code that you will find in an envelope inside your mailbox. Sister will explain more."

"Thanks, Sal." Noah and I said in unison. This was definitely strange. I was glad to make it to the parking lot without incident and gladder still when Noah helped me from the car, shielding me from a view of the athletic building.

"Oh, no," I said under my breath, when I saw that Ken Telford's funny little hybrid was already here. At least the windows weren't fogged up, which I took to be a good sign. Dolores and Sister Paul were had also arrived and I let out a more colorful phrase than 'oh no,' when I recalled the Honor's folder was still in the trunk of my car.

"I forgot Dolores' folder," I told Noah as we headed for the path.

"Do you want to go back and get it? It's still early."

I thought for a moment but did not relish seeing more people on our return trip. I knew there was nothing wrong with receiving a lift from Noah, but I still wanted to keep our new friendship to myself.

"No, I'll just bring it tomorrow. If she doesn't come find me, Dolores and I do not really cross paths."

It was early enough that Jeremy Wrobleski would be using a lamp in his office, so I felt free to walk up the path without worry when I saw the window dark. A few more cars were scattered in the lot, including Scott Pearson's of course, but we met no one in the faculty room.

A delightful surprise, which Sal neglected to mention, was that my key card also had my picture on it. Knowing that mine looked like me, as a photograph will, I was still dismayed at how strange I appeared. The picture was from a year book photo of some year's past, so I was not surprised to learn that Noah's card bore none yet.

Without giving each other the full codes we ascertained that we each had a different one. I wondered how this all worked. Did some security program, perhaps now located in Sister Paul's office, register the entrance of specific people?

"We should check upstairs." Noah said this with more curiosity than trepidation and I was once again reminded how a long time teacher here would feel the strangeness of these changes more so than someone recently arrived.

But when we reached my single classroom door, nothing new and high tech marred it. Poor Noah had to hold both of our coffees and my bag aloft, while I frantically searched its pockets for my keys. I was glad that the long weekend did not afford time to change the old fashioned key holes. I loved my heavy, filigreed key and planned to ask to keep it when the time came for it to be decommissioned.

"I'm walking to physical therapy this afternoon, can I get this back to you tomorrow?" I waved my coffee mug, which was still half full.

"Absolutely. I probably should have done this in the car, because it feels a bit strange now, but can I have your phone number?"

It did feel strange to write my number down on one of my silly sticky pads, but not in a bad way.

"I cannot thank you enough. You seem to know me well for someone I just met."

"I told you," he said with a warm smile, "I pay attention."

Watching him leave, my own smile transitioned from delighted to something more determined. Once my grades were entered, I decided to walk across to the guidance office to ask Toni Anne Tancredi a few questions. As nearly as I could tell, the other women of the guidance department were not here yet, but Toni Anne was likely to be, given that Ken was. I wanted my questions about Laurie Boone's transcript to be heard by as few people as possible.

Taking only my cane and key, I stealthily made my way from the building, only belatedly hoping that Sal had left the main door of the Towers open today as well. My own ears were acutely attuned to sound, as the last thing I wanted was to draw any attention from the administrative offices up stairs. But Laurie's situation was weighing on me and I was fairly certain it had its place in the puzzle of Tim's murder. Before I tried to explain the byzantine workings of our school to Detective Lawson, I wanted proof that the unfair honors program placements were more than just clerical errors.

I knocked on the guidance office door, which generally remained open during the school day. An appliquéd pillow hung on the closed door, festooned with the phrase, "knowledge is power." I was thinking about that when I heard a man's voice from behind the door. Since swiveling was not really possible, I backed away, like a car in the midst of a k-turn, and fled.

It had never occurred to me that Ken and Toni Anne would be as foolhardy as to hide together in her office. Actually, it had not occurred to me that Toni Anne would be, as a guidance counselor and a long term employee here. Ken already strutted about like the common rules of behavior did not apply to him and this was the second time I had very nearly caught them.

Sighing at their folly and my own risky, wasted trip, I returned to the safety of my classroom. Taking a few minutes to just breathe in the calming scent of lavender, I set about organizing my journals and tests. Happy work, this kept me thoroughly occupied until the homeroom bell sounded.

As the lowest on the school's hierarchy, the freshmen in my homeroom did not know very much about Tim's murder and were not particularly interested. Their questions, asked of both me and each other, centered about how the loss of two days would affect their future schedules. I tried to assure them that their teachers would not treat this alteration as a punishable occurrence.

"Yo, Ms. Lake." Frankie DiMeo stood large in the doorway, my entire class silencing at his arrival.

"Johnny M. is going to meet you after school, I have to help my dad move some stuff."

"No worries, Frankie. I am walking today but thanks for letting me know. And make sure you get that recommendation form to me soon."

Nodding at me briefly, Frankie growled at my kids before bounding away. Taking stock of their reactions, I noticed some looked impressed, a few afraid. A few of the girls looked all together different. Adding to my mental list of worries, I vowed to have a conversation with Mr. DiMeo about what dating pools he should swim in.

A moment later, another senior appeared. Luckily this one took no notice of my homeroom or barely any of me. We had a service program for those students who received demerits, and clearly this young man was not laboring by choice.

Homeroom, it seemed, was being extended so that Sister Paul could explain the new security measures to the staff and students. The upper classes would be going to the auditorium immediately while the sophomores and freshmen would wait in homeroom. The upper classes would then wait in homeroom when it was time for the underclassmen to go down to auditorium. To accommodate all this, first period would not be meeting.

I glanced over at my wall calendar, reminding myself that this was now an "E" day in our schedule system, to account for the loss of Monday. I took a deep breath, if I were to explain all of this to my worried little group, I had better get started.

Our new security protocols, a phrase that was not mine, were still the primary topic of conversation as my senior Honors group made their way to their seats. I had looked for Laurie, as they shuffled in, though hardly expecting to see her. In their present moods, the return of the summer reading exams was a bit anticlimactic. Though they knew the drill from previous years, I still explained how this grade would be calculated and cautioned them to expect questions about these readings throughout the year.

Chatter resumed as they were putting their journals away and I was readying my computer screen. No matter how well motivated a class might be, I had never successfully schooled anyone in the quiet transition from one activity to the next.

The general consensus seemed to be that the safety changes were pointless and inconvenient. I jumped into the fray, believing it my duty to sell these students on the necessity of the system.

"We are really only talking about some locked doors and a passes to better monitor you while you are outside the classroom. Frankly, most schools I know of already have both of these protocols." I did hate myself a bit for using the word protocols.

"But Ms. Lake, this is all so hypocritical." Tiffany Ferguson, an editor of the school newspaper, thought everything that went on here was hypocritical. Given what I had been learning the past few days, I looked at her with curiosity.

"We are all going to be under a microscope during the day but what about after? The teams will just run wild, like they always do when the teachers leave."

I shushed a few members of sporting teams, who took umbrage at her remarks but needn't have bothered. The look Tiffany threw around the room had made even me take a step back. She was also correct. Sister Paul had made no mention of how security would be increased before and after the school day, an odd omission, considering when and where Tim had been killed.

"I am sure the Athletic Director will be speaking to the teams." As I spoke, I picked up my copy of *Hamlet* to indicate that this topic had come to a close. I desperately wanted to call out the person who had made a derisive snort at my comment, but I was unsure who it was. I also did not want to participate in any gossip about the Athletic Director though I found the implied criticism interesting, given that I never heard a positive or negative word about Nick Morrison.

"Now when we left Hamlet, he had just suffered the shock of his father's visitation. How can we consider this the defining moment in Hamlet's life?"

And so we spent a satisfying half hour discussing Hamlet's complex dilemma. I was gratified to see almost complete investment in the story, which, when removed from the more melodramatic elements, was the struggle of a young man against the loss of all he had trusted in.

We ended, a bit too fittingly, at the line, "that one may smile, and smile, and be a villain."

"Who would like to explain, Tiffany?"

"Hamlet is realizing that people lie and betray you, and they can be smiling while they do it." Tiffany's tone suggested she had already made this discovery.

"How does Hamlet react to this discovery, knowing already that his uncle has murdered his father?"

"Hamlet hates his uncle," Johnny Marchiano offered. "And his mother."

"He is disgusted too." Marie Demarest added.

"At whom?"

"At them, but also at himself."

I thought Marie's comment an interesting one to pursue and gestured for her to explain. Looking around the room, I saw that everyone was still attentive.

"Hamlet was like everyone else when they're young. He was blind. If he hadn't been so horrified when his mother married his uncle, maybe he would never have realized how many villains smiled at him."

"Ignorance is bliss."

I looked over at Johnny, who continued.

"Was he better off knowing that his uncle was a murderer and his mother was involved? We all know how this is going to end. If the truth is going to get you killed, wouldn't you rather not know?"

The bell rang when he was speaking, so the question hung there for a moment, with the ghost of Tim Boone dancing around it. The class shuffled out, much more quietly than they had entered. I forgot to assign them their homework.

"You're walking home, Ms. Lake?" Johnny had lingered and I expected there were things he wanted to talk about.

"Actually, I am walking, but to physical therapy."

Audrey had called me late in the afternoon yesterday to tell me that Tim's partner had arranged for a replacement therapist to come down from Binghamton. I had not even been aware that Tim had a business partner. I was newly struck by how little Tim said about himself in all the months I had known him.

"Laurie isn't coming to school for a while."

I nodded, wondering if she could ever come back to the site of her father's murder. My anger at Tim's killer grew again. To Johnny, I said,

"This cannot be easy for her but she is lucky to have you."

Johnny brushed aside this compliment, no doubt in the way he dismissed his own mother's praise. Boys were like that.

"Do you think Mr. Boone was a villain?" He asked me.

Briefly taken aback by this, I only pointed out that Tim had been the victim of a crime, not the perpetrator.

"Yeah, but getting killed doesn't mean you were innocent of everything. The guys have been saying that most people don't just get killed, that Mr. Boone had to be into something, like drugs."

There was that phrase again. Brian had also said that Tim was 'into a lot of things.' I was still trying to determine what that meant.

"First of all," I said, "Mr. Boone was a physical therapist, not a doctor. He didn't have any more access to drugs than you or I."

As I spoke, I immediately thought of Angry Cop and wondered if Detective Lawson had pursued that business about Tim getting weight loss pills from him. I hoped none of my uncertainty showed upon my face.

"I know that, Ms. Lake, and the really dumb stuff doesn't bother me. I've heard that Coach killed him, or you did since you're the one that found him, or I did it."

I chose to ignore Johnny's first two enumerated suspects. It was natural he would side, perhaps blindly, with his coach. I was hardly surprised that the kids knew I had found Tim's body. If the faculty knew something, the kids would too.

"You?"

"Like I was mad because Mr. Boone wanted me to stop seeing Laurie. I'm on scholarship."

His last statement was no non sequitur. This was primarily a school for the children of the wealthy. It was naïve to assume that differences in money and status went unnoticed. But I had always assumed that Johnny's abilities and character ameliorated any prejudice against him. I was sick to learn otherwise.

"Whoever said that is a fool." I wanted to use stronger language, but Johnny was a student, so I abstained.

"I don't care, Ms. Lake, whatever. And Mr. Boone was always nice to me and really interested in where I was applying. He wanted Laurie and me to go to the same school if we could."

"Yet," I prompted. Johnny had come to me because he was worried that Tim was a villain. There was more he wanted to say.

"Mr. Boone was always asking questions," he began. I was once again struck by how Johnny was confirming something that I had already been told. Audrey also noted how curious Tim could be about some things. 'He was funny about money,' she had said.

"Laurie would joke about it sometimes, that he was always asking her questions about her friend's parents, her teachers, people at school. Then he would ask me and the guys when he worked out here. What did we know about the coach? Where did the stuff the coach gave us came from?"

Johnny took a breath and I could tell that he had been wrestling with the things he had just begun to notice, as I had.

"Before I knew it, guys would be confessing all this stuff, because Mr. Boone seemed so nice and was good about our evaluations. Who heard about somebody scamming or somebody whose parents were splitting up. We are here pretty late too and you do see stuff, even with teachers. He had us starting to notice things for him. It was weird."

"Johnny," I said. "If you haven't told Detective Lawson about this I think you should."

"Nah, Ms. Lake I guess I already have. Me and a few of the guys. But now it sounds like Mr. Boone was doing something wrong. And did I betray Laurie, like everybody betrayed Hamlet? What if she won't trust me again?"

"Johnny, listen hon. I am sure Laurie wants her father's killer caught. When that happens she will have to learn things about her him that she would rather not know. But that is out of everyone's hands, yours included. It's going to be a long recovery and Laurie will have a lot to deal with, but you can be there for her and help her. It is not you who has betrayed her trust."

131

Johnny stood for a moment with his head bowed, but he was smiling when he looked up.

"Thanks, Ms. Lake. I knew you would understand."

"And I am here to help. You make sure you let Laurie know too."

"Ok, I can carry your bag down, before I go lift?"

"No, I am fine, sweetie. Just help me straighten these rows out."

I finished my classroom cleaning after Johnny left, my thoughts more heavy than they had even been this morning. Checking that I had my new key card and my own special code, I headed out to therapy. I hoped to find more answers there.

As it happened, a potential answer followed me into the work-out room, about twenty minutes after my arrival. I suspected Toni Anne was less than pleased to see me but was effectively trapped. Audrey had informed me that the new therapist was running behind, and we would be here for a while.

"Hey," I said, by way of non-threatening greeting. "Can I ask you a question?"

Toni Anne looked a bit askance, but what could she do? I had trouble imagining anyone with the temerity to respond, that no, they would not be asked any questions. Amending my own thought, I realized Angry Cop could probably do it with ease.

"What is it?"

I was on the exercise bike, and could lean only so much in her direction without tipping off, so I lowered my voice as much as I dared.

"Do you know how Laurie Boone got into the Honors Program this year?"

Looking slightly relieved, before becoming quizzical, Toni Anne asked me what I meant.

"Her transcript is excellent," she said."I was surprised she was never in the program before."

"Did you ask any of the other guidance counselor about her?"

Toni Anne monitored only the seniors, I doubted she would have had reason to see Laurie's transcript before.

"Why would I?"

Deciding that my continued perusal of this required I share with her some details, told her about the Honors Committee Dolores had created, imagining that Toni Anne had not been paying much mind at the faculty meeting.

"Laurie and a few other students in the program had transcripts with much, much lower averages than are permissible. These were regular looking transcripts, given to me by Dolores."

"I am not sure what to say, Addra. I just had Laurie's in my hand today. I wanted to make sure her file was in order, because she might not be here for all the preliminary stuff with do with college applications. She had near a hundred average."

She just stared at me. I checked my time on the bicycle, and decided I had done enough.

Getting off carefully, I went to sit next to Toni Anne, who was using an exercise board to strengthen her ankle. I took a deep breath.

"I think Tim bribed or blackmailed someone at the school to alter his daughter's transcript. Do you think that's possible?"

Toni Anne reeled back from me, as though I had threatened her.

"You don't think…"

"No," I answered quickly. I did not think she had done it. I was not even sure, as guidance counselor, she could. But I did think she knew a bit about Tim and secrets.

"But Tim knew you and Ken Telford are having an affair, right?"

I could not believe I had actually said that and was not even sure I was correct until I saw the color leave Toni Anne's face. Randomly, I was struck by how I had

133

never witnessed such a thing, though it was described often enough in books. She really did look utterly bloodless.

"What did he want to keep silent?"

This was another guess on my part, but it also stood to reason. I had been hearing for days that Tim was very interested in certain types of knowledge. Taken with the proof that someone had doctored his daughter's grades, it was an easy leap to the notion of blackmail. Easy to surmise at least, I was having great difficulty with the idea that Tim could have been so corrupted and calculating.

"Nothing terrible, Addra, just help. He wanted me to help Laurie, with her college applications." I just looked at her, with an admittedly tense glare. Though my track record had suffered of late, I could still spot a liar, especially when they lied this poorly.

"I was going to have to write her admissions essays, doctor her teacher recommendations and, pad her applications. I process everything. All their applications are in my hands last."

"But that's fraud." I breathed, immediately regretting my own expression of naiveté. I had been so collected up until this point. I was also speaking to an admitted adulterer, willing to be blackmailed into a crime just to continue her affair.

"Have you told Detective Lawson this?"

"How could I? It could get back to Ken's wife and would definitely get back to the school."

To myself I wondered how concerned Toni Anne could really be if she was constantly meeting with Ken on school grounds. To her I said,

"You have to tell him. You were not the only person Tim was blackmailing. It must have to do with his murder." I refused to bandy about words like motive and means. I would feel entirely too much like Mrs. Marple.

"I can't. I can't."

Toni Anne was frantic but I would not allow myself any sympathy, not while Laurie Boone and her mother went to sleep knowing Tim's killer was still out there.

"You have to Toni Anne, or I will."

I stood up, deciding I needed to get out of there, even without seeing the new therapist. I would just tell Audrey I was not feeling well. If she glanced over at Toni Anne she may well conclude that something serious was going around the school.

"Hey, Audrey, I am going to head out."

"I know Addra, I am sorry the wait is so long. Could you try tomorrow? I know it won't be such a squeeze."

"Sure, that would be great." It was even better that I was not compelled to lie.

"Oh, hey, before you go—could I give you this? It was lying around here for a few days before I could remember what it was."

She held up a lone key, dangling from a rabbit's foot key chain. I remember Tim telling me he purchased the silly thing because Laurie's favorite color was pink and she always brought him luck. It was the key Tim used to get into the St. Augustine athletic building.

"Audrey," said in a quiet voice. "You need to call Detective Lawson."

She looked startled.

"Why?"

"If Tim left his key here, then it could mean that somebody from the school let him in. Nobody has said they did."

"So the person who let him in could have killed him?"

I did not want to be too overdramatic. Perhaps all the focus upon Coach Brown and his habits was because the detectives had already determined that the door had been left open after practice the night before.

"Not necessarily, but it is still important to determining the circumstances of Tim's death."

I was not sure what I was talking about, but Audrey seemed duly impressed.

"I'll call right now," she said, reaching for the phone.

Though I had no reason to believe Detective Lawson was on the corner, waiting for her call, I still exited with alacrity, and looked around every turn before descending the stairs.

I was already home, and in my pajamas, before two, much belated thoughts occurred to me. Ken Telford could have killed Tim for threatening to expose his and Toni Anne's affair. And, more frighteningly, I should not have threatened to do the same.

Before I could reconsider, I went to find my cordless phone and dialed Noah's number, which I had managed to memorize, despite only dialing it once before.

"Noah?"

"Addra, hi. I was just thinking about you."

Noah sounded calm and safe.

"Noah, do you think you could drive me to work tomorrow? Any time you want."

"Sure I can. What time are you walking?"

"Oh, I'm not walking tomorrow. Any time you want is fine."

"Ok. But is something wrong? You sound funny."

I had forgotten that Noah was a mind reader.

"Well, I'm probably just being silly. But, I discovered that two people at school are having an affair, and one of them was being blackmailed by Tim. I insisted that the woman tell the detectives, because it has to be related to his murder."

I paused, allowing Noah to ask,

"You're expecting that this couple were not the only people being blackmailed?"

"Exactly. But after I told her that I would tell the detectives about her, if she didn't—"

"You said that?"

"Yes. But it wasn't until later, that I wondered if the man she was having the affair with killed Tim, and—"

"And you had just threatened to expose them." I could hear Noah's sigh.

"Yeah. Do you think I'm being silly?" I tried to laugh but didn't quite pull it off. I was amazed that I had just laid this all before him, a testimony to my fear.

"No, you are not being silly. And you need to call the detectives."

He was right; I would be calling Detective Lawson next.

"Ok. Thank you, Noah."

He murmured a few things, before I hung up the phone.

This time I went to get my cell phone, also not thinking too deeply about why I had programmed Detective Lawson's number into it. Once again, I was forced to leave a message.

"Listen, Detective Lawson, I have something to tell you. Well, a few things. Two people at St. Augustine's are having an affair, Toni Anne Tancredi and Ken Telford. Tim was blackmailing Toni Anne into manufacturing better college applications for his daughter. Also, I have semi-proof that Tim got someone at school to change his daughter's transcript and make her grades better. I don't know who. This is Addra Lake."

I hung up, with my head in my hands. I should have taken more time to collect my thoughts before committing such an awkward message to permanence. I would have stayed there, my embarrassment warring with my fear, had the doorbell not rung.

Looking through the peephole first, I saw Noah. When I opened the door, I saw the bag in his hand.

"I parked up the block," he said, by way of greeting. I let him in.

Chapter Nine

Early the next morning, Detective Lawson returned my call. I was evidently surrounded by men who never provided me with a proper greeting because he opened with,

"Are you doing my job for me, Ms. Lake?" He did not sound angry, but I was still thoroughly intimidated. To cover this, I chose the offensive.

"No," I yelled, belatedly remembering that Noah was still sleeping in my living room.

"People have just been talking to me," I whispered. "And I had to tell you. I'm not gossiping Detective."

"I know that, Ms. Lake. And I cannot tell you about the investigation, but I do appreciate your information, and it is substantiating some things we've been learning. I am going to have to speak to some people at your school again."

"Thanks for returning my call Detective." I was calming down a bit.

"And be careful, Ms. Lake." He hung up, and I was immediately nervous again.

"Hey," Noah said, looking positively adorable in his plaid pajama pants and tee shirt. His hair was what you'd expect from someone who spent the night on a strange sofa but he wore it well.

"Hey," I answered, "that was Detective Lawson. He thanked me for the information but didn't say much beyond that it confirmed what they were already thinking. He did say he would be coming back to school."

"I'm sure they can keep your name out of it."

I looked at him for a long moment.

"I doubt it, since I just told Toni Anne everything I knew. Plus this business with changing Laurie Boone's grades, only you, I, and Dolores knew about that. I don't want any of this to come back to you." Worry about Dolores' reprisal had been one of the myriad of things keeping me awake last night since it seemed likely she never shared the information with the detectives.

I had crept around into the early hours, making the bathroom company ready and mixing up a breakfast casserole and scones. Even now, at six in the morning, I had already showered and dressed. Only men looked good when they were rumpled.

"If you want to take a shower, breakfast will be out of the oven in fifteen minutes. I left you towels."

Since I was unsure how to handle this acceleration in our nascent relationship, I was morphing into the proprietor of a bread and breakfast. I handed him his coffee, poured into a fancy china cup. He accepted it, put it down on the counter, and pulled me close. Closing my eyes, I imagined I would have slept better if we had been thus last night.

"Did you sleep at all last night?" He asked into my hair.

"A bit," I said honestly. "But it really helped to have you here."

And it had, providing me with a shiny, new set of worries. If given a choice, who wouldn't abandon fear of retaliatory death for the worry a man we liked might notice how infrequently we dusted? It was arguable how much actual protection Noah had provided though, sleeping like a log. Ken Telford could have entered my home with a battering ram and I doubted Noah would have stirred.

When he returned, dressed for work in enviably unwrinkled clothes, I had the table set and the food adorning it.

"I can't believe you did all this for me." He said, sitting.

I refused to tell him how glad I was to have him here to do all this for. I had not been in relationship for a long while and obviously none of my past ones had ended well. I had grown accustomed to ignoring my loneliness but with Noah here, it was hard.

"It seems strange to think we might work with a murderer."

"Really? I assumed Stan Grimm was a mass murderer the first time I met him."

139

I laughed, since I thought the same, more than once.

"Straying from the topic of murder for a minute, may I ask you about Parent Information Night? Specifically what I have to do?"

I groaned, putting my buttered scone down, before I threw it. Though I had more excuse than usual to be distracted, I was miffed at myself for forgetting all about this. Besides having to go to physical therapy right after class, I and the other faculty were expected back at school by 7:30.

"There is not much too it, if you are in the mood for it," I began, clearly signally that I was far from the appropriate one.

"Each department and major activity has an information table set up in the gym. Sister Paul and Dolores usually give speeches, coffee and pastries are set out and then the parents just mingle about, asking questions."

"What do we do?"

"Well, the chair people usually helm the actual information tables, so the faculty just mill around, looking approachable."

"Is there usually a good turn out?"

I thought for a moment.

"There certainly will be tonight. I don't envy Sister Paul's job fielding all the inevitable questions about Tim's murder. Otherwise, it is what you would expect. Most of the freshman parents come. The Honors Program parents, of all grades, always have a lot of questions and then a smattering from the each grade. Once you start to go through the year, you will start to recognize the really participatory parents."

We had been clearing the table while talking and I was enjoying how economical Noah's movements were. A mostly unbidden image of living with him floated into my mind, turning my face red. I prayed he would not ask me about it, since I seemed to always tell him the unvarnished truth.

He took my bag from me at the door, and kissed me once before exiting. I sighed and followed.

All day long I waited for an announcement that Parent Information Night had been cancelled, though I knew no such luck would be mine. I also knew what a public relations nightmare it would have been to deny the parents their right to ask questions about the safety of the school.

I was unsure how much more safe it was, but I could attest to how exhausting I found this new key card system. The act of using it required no real effort, only in my case, forgetting it in my classroom required retracing my steps several times throughout the day.

On one of those occasions I had been attempting to bring Dolores' folder back, having rescued it from my trunk before Noah drove us in this morning. But when I entered the administrative area, no one was there. Immediately my thoughts returned to that terrible Friday, now six days past, when I had gone to be questioned by Detective Lawson for the first time.

I wondered if that was where the secretaries were now, though it was more likely that last minute preparations for Information Night had led them from their desks. Unwilling to do anything with this folder, save depositing it directly into Dolores's hands, I had returned it to my classroom before cutting across the lawn.

I was walking to therapy, having turned down Noah's offer of a ride, to make up for the lack of exercise this morning. Thereafter I had to high tail it home, throw down some leftovers, and make myself presentable before Ginny picked me up at 7:15.

Heading down the alley, I noticed that the ground had been swept and no cigarette butts remained. I could still see the black marks along the alley wall. At this time, so soon after dismissal, I might have expected to run into a student or two, but Sister had made it quite clear that the kids were to leave the campus post haste. All clubs and team activities had also been suspended for the day.

Our maintenance staff consisted entirely of Sal, and he was essentially being asked to clean the entire campus for a second time today, and then for a third, when the parents left.

Stepping from the alley, I was gladdened to see that a number of trees had realized that autumn was upon them. Their bright colors bolstered my failing energy and I walked past my accident site with hardly a twinge.

I was even happy to see Mr. Delgado, knowing any conversation with him would be short.

"Hi Mr. Delgado, aren't the trees beautiful?" I lifted my free arm to sweep across the sight.

"Trees mean leaves, Addra. Leaves are a scourge."

I expected him to say something like that, but chose to also be heartened that this expectation had proven correct. It was a fine thing that Mr. Delgado thought leaves a scourge. Leaves had a way of falling and this curmudgeonly old man needed something to occupy his time. The six bags already on his lawn testified to this symbiosis.

"Any luck with the pooper?" I asked.

"Not yet, but the camera goes all night, so I have a lot to get through. I'm going to catch him, you wait."

Informing him I was more than happy to wait, I continued on my way. Tim's murder may have purged away some of my delight in my fellow faculty, but I was bolstered to recall the new friends that I had made this year, not least of which, was Mr. Delgado. I said a silent prayer to God, and threw in an extra one for the pooper, who I knew would rue the day he had not scooped.

Entering the overly warm therapy office, I was relieved to see that Audrey had been right. The place was completely empty, as far as I could tell.

Walking into the reception area to sign in, I smelled a distinctly floral perfume, prompting me to ask if the new physical therapist was a woman.

"Her name is Barbara," Audrey said quietly, with no inflection.

"What is she like?"

"She's nice. Professional."

It was an interesting dictment against Tim, seeing as she had never appeared unhappy to work for him in the time I had known her. But why, I asked myself, do you continue to take what seems to be as proof of what is? This week had proven me wrong about so many things.

As I bicycled my four miles to nowhere, a line from *Hamlet* fittingly repeated in my mind. "Seems, madam? Nay, it is. I know not seems." I was glad to see I never failed to be buoyed by an apt quotation.

Otherwise, I was physically sinking under the weight of too little sleep and my pedaling threatened to come to a complete halt. The thought of returning to work made me want to curl up in a ball and weep.

"The police came to pick up Tim's key." Audrey spoke out of the corner of her mouth, quietly, as she straightened the neat rows of ankle weights. The very professional Barbara must not like fraternization with the patients.

"They asked a lot of questions about Dougie," she continued.

I found that interesting but was still bothered by the keys. If Angry Cop were the killer I could surmise that Tim had let him in to the athletic building. But how had Tim gained entrance that morning if his keys were here? The whole thing turned on Coach Brown or Nick Morrison leaving the building unlocked after practice the night before.

That was certainly a possibility, given the nervous way I had seen Mike Brown behave, but, if they were anything like myself when I misplaced something, we would never know for sure. The entire reason one frets over the possibility of leaving a door unlocked is specifically because one has no recollection of either locking it or leaving it open. I was concerned this aspect of Tim's murder might never be definitively solved.

About twenty minutes later, the new therapist Barbara, emerged from behind one of the treatment room curtains, followed by a patient I had seen a few times. I was shocked, given how I had not heard a single sound come from that direction.

Beckoning me to follow her, Barbara indicated that she had already read my file, so I had no need to explain my case to her. Dutifully lying down, we exchanged no other words, save for her giving me a few directions. Her grip was stronger than even Tim's had been.

"I feel like I have been hit by a car." I said to Audrey, as I took my leave.

She returned my bitter smile with one of her own, "Well, you should be used to that by now."

Snorting, I walked out, all in all, in the perfect mood to return to work.

"Why are these things never on a Friday?" Ginny asked, as we pulled into the sports lot, off of 9th street.

"Because none of the parents would come?" I offered.

As I had predicted to Noah this morning, concern over Tim's murder had produced a record turn-out for Information Night. This resulted in Ginny and I being unable to find a spot in the main parking lot. As such, we would be walking across the Athletic Complex to reach the academic building, something I was loathe to do.

Luckily, Ginny kept up a steady stream of chatter as we walked which provided background noise, if not any useful information. She had her customary litany of complaints, about Mark, about her husband, her own kids, as well as the hundred or so kids she taught. They were her typical quibbles, and I marveled at her total lack of interest in Tim's murder before realizing that there was much about it she did not know.

Funny, I had kept my promises of silence to both Dolores and Detective Lawson, excepting my full disclosure with Noah. To him, I just wanted to tell the truth. It was strange, events had catapulted us past all the usual pitter patter of dating, but we had also not demarcated any lines in our relationship. How circumspect should we be while at work? As I had flippantly told him, neither one of us were married. But all the same, I think I wanted our feelings to remain private while doubting that would be possible.

When Ginny and I entered the lobby of the academic building, it was 7:25. Knowing Sister Paul as we did, it was necessary to push past an alarming number of people to reach the table earmarked for the English department. She usually began her welcome speech by introducing the faculty. Mark was already there.

"Ken's not coming." He said this with no particular tone, adding, "he only started during the summer program any way, and doesn't know much."

"Truer words were never spoken," I muttered under my breath.

Ginny was not satisfied with Mark's reaction and said so.

"Let it go, Ginny. Sister knows."

The finality of that statement quieted Ginny, for now. Feeling the stirrings of guilt, despite my best efforts, I sought out Toni Anne. Seated at the first of the two tables given to the Guidance department, I could all but feel her dismay from across the room. Detective Lawson had evidently made good on his promise to pursue what I had learned. Did that make me safe? Was Ken in jail?

I next sought Noah, and was warmed to catch him already in the act of looking for me. We both smiled and I could all but feel that as well.

Turning my eyes away from the processional that Sister Paul once again led, I hoped that Anne Boone had not attended.

Jeremy Wrobleski was allowed to lead the prayer, which I ignored. Sister did introduce each member of the faculty and I was horrified to find myself blushing when Noah's name was called.

"Are you ok?" Ginny asked. "You look weird."

After the last smattering of polite applause faded, Sister Paul took a deep breath and began.

"Each year, of my thirty years here, Parent Information Night provided our first link in the chain of connection, between you, the parents of our charges, and us, who work with you to provide your children with the finest education possible. But this year is different. St. Augustine's has been the site of a terrible crime and we have lost one of our most valued parents."

I wondered how many on the faculty could tell that Sister was not being altogether truthful. She betrayed this with slightest twitch in her right eye. It was a useful thing to know and I had thanked Ginny many times for telling me.

"As I have already explained to you in a letter, the school has augmented its security measures in several key areas. All entrances and exits have cameras upon them, as well as in each of the parking lots. The doors have keyless entry, with cards that are marked by their user. We are able to monitor who is in the buildings at all times."

I looked into the audience to see how this information was being received. Many parents were nodding, seemingly at ease. But one man was waving his arms in a belligerent fashion, belligerent to me, because Sister was not yet done speaking.

"Yes, sir?" She asked, graciously.

"Are we going to see all these upgrades paid for by a tuition hike?"

I heard Joe Torres' snort, clear as a bell, from his perch next to the tiny table labeled art. I had assumed concern over the murder itself might prompt some heated questions, but once again the failure of my perceptions left me speechless.

"No sir, I assure you that adequate funding has been ear marked for these improvements, in such a way that shall not impact the tuition or any of our existing programs and services."

"How is that possible?" Ginny asked in my ear.

I had no idea, but I wondered if Sister Paul's yearly redecorating budget had borne the burden. She took her role as custodian of St. Augustine's very seriously and would consider her loss a justified one.

"The investigation into Mr. Boone's death is still ongoing but I have been told, just today, that progress is being made and an arrest is expected shortly. I am happy to speak to anyone with further concerns, but I now invite you to view our presentations, meet with your children's teachers, and enjoy what refreshments you wish."

I watched Sister walk into the fray, her small stature soon making her invisible from view. The initial minutes of Parent Information Night were always a bit awkward, as I tried to keep a countenance of helpful interest upon my face while being essentially at a loss for what to say. I was much better answering questions in a classroom than I was at striking up conversation.

"Ms. Lake?" An amiable looking couple stood before me.

"We're Monica and Seth Tunstill, Seth's parents."

They stood expectantly, as parents tended to do after introducing themselves. Luckily Seth had already made an impression.

"Your son is a very serious young man and extraordinarily polite," I began. "You must be proud."

His mother answered with a smile.

"We are, though we are hoping he becomes a bit more relaxed as he grows more comfortable here."

Her husband, the elder Seth, continued.

"And we appreciate the way you answer all his questions and explain how the school operates. Seth needs that kind of clarity."

It was true, little Seth wrote down everything I said, and I was only his homeroom teacher. But he had another small freshman that he exited my room with each morning, and in the beginning of a new school year, that was usually enough.

After a few more pleasantries, which were truly pleasant, the Tunstill's drifted away, holding each other's hands. I immediately thought of Noah, and moved to find him. He was in conversation with the father of a junior member of the Honors Program. I knew Mr. Pagano well, from my interactions with him in the first semester of last year, and was glad to be able to rescue Noah.

"Mr. Pagano, how are you?"

"Ms. Lake. I am happy to see you here. That woman who replaced you last year did not impress my Lawrence at all."

I easily recalled how rudely Lawrence expressed his disappointment, according to the Dean, Susan Mullen. Air borne papers had figured largely. But Mr. Pagano was a parent who only recognized flaws outside of his own home, and that was unlikely to change.

"Well, I hope to see Larry in my class next year." I smiled, in diplomatic fashion, before resting my hand on Noah's arm.

"Mr. Stabler, I was wondering if you could help me get a case of water from the storage closet."

Not betraying a single quizzical glance, Noah extricated himself from Mr. Pagano and let me lead him out of the gymnasium and into the relative quiet of the lobby.

"The cafeteria staff is handling refreshments." He muttered.

"But Mr. Pagano would be trying to handle you for the next hour."

By mutual consent, we walked towards the exit, for a few moments of private conversation. It was a lovely night, cool enough for me to enjoy the chill. We sat on one of the stone benches, while I spared my usual prayer for the monks who once inhabited this school.

"I noticed Ken is not in attendance." Noah said. I had told him last night exactly whom I feared.

"And Toni Anne looks as sick as a dog. Detective Lawson must have paid them a visit."

Thinking for a long moment, I added.

"I wonder how all that is going to shake out."

"Is the administration really that interested in the private lives of their teachers?" Noah had arrived here from a metropolitan public school, I reminded myself. I also wondered what had brought him to this school, and asked.

"Late night internet search," he smiled.

"When you are miserable, drastic change holds the most appeal. I'm an only child and my parents retired to Phoenix. I would be far from them staying in Boston or living here."

I pointed out that I too, was an only child.

Picking up the thread of his original conversation, I continued.

"I think that the issue is not with two teachers pursuing a relationship, though I doubt Sister Paul would be thrilled with the gossip that would incur. It's the fact that Ken is married and they didn't seem to do a good job of hiding it."

We were silent again, but it was a companionable one. There were many reasons I liked Noah, not least of which was the fact that he didn't fill the air with empty words.

"I want to see you Addra and I don't really want to hide it. I can resist groping you in the hallways, but I don't want to pretend I don't look for you in every room I enter."

I took his hand, and enjoyed its warmth for a moment, before saying,

"Me too. How I feel about you is the only uncomplicated thing about the last few weeks. I really appreciate last night too." I needed to say that one final time, half hoping that Noah would try to convince me that danger still existed, so he would stay longer.

"You have no reason to thank me." He stood.

"I'll walk in first. Call me when you get home?"

I smiled my assent and watched him go. I only heard the footfall when I bent to retrieve my cane. A whispered voice said,

"He was already here."

I expected nothing but darkness by the time I turned around and darkness was what I found.

Thinking furiously but futilely, I returned to the academic building. I was not afraid, which was the most peculiar thing, but took my visitor's words as a warning, signaling that I was still missing something essential to Tim's murder. As an English teacher I was also vexed that most of my confusion hung on my whisperer's use of a pronoun. I try to teach the kids to identify their nouns, but nobody ever listens.

The faculty room was located directly beyond the lobby, and I went there, expecting it to be empty. It was not.

Bernadette, the secretary I strongly suspected had changed Laurie Boone's grades, was putting small objects into cloth bags, emblazoned with the St. Augustine's logo. Gift bags for the parents; the modern education system had become one long swag party.

Having recently believed Ken Telford might kill me, I was not intimidated by Bernadette's glare. The woman was barely five feet tall, and of some indeterminate age decades beyond mine.

"Here to check on me?" She asked, throwing a roll of ribbon down upon the table.

"No," I answered with honest vehemence. The faculty room door emptied directly into the room, with no hallway to hide one's decision to turn around unnoticed. I did not want to be here, having been the one to alert the Detective Lawson of Laurie Boone's grade change and another possible motive in Tim's murder.

I approached the table and began to prop open more gift bags, readying them for the small clocks, calendars, and mints that were to go in them, all with the same gold stamp of the school. I imagined that these things alone could have paid for a good deal of security. Bernadette watched me work for a moment, but did not stop me.

"They're getting their last bit of blood out of me before tomorrow." She spoke bitterly.

"Tomorrow?" I asked, while knowing what she would say next.

"Sister Paul thinks I changed those Honors kid's grades."

I noticed she admitted nothing, which I supposed was savvy, given my track record of talking to Detective Lawson. But I was still livid. Academic honesty was sacrosanct. The only thing to excuse the cheating of students was their age. A school could not survive if word that it's employees altered transcripts got out. I thought of college scholarships, and beyond them, student's actual futures, compromised.

To Bernadette, I only said,

"What was Tim holding over you?"

She gave me a look signifying her opinion of my interrogation methods.

"You teachers all think your jobs are hard. I hear you complain, all time, you complain. Think of my job. You have to know your one subject and your own students. I have to keep track of every student, and every subject, and every date, and every rule." She paused for a breath, and I prayed, to put down the clock she held, before it smashed in her clenched hands.

"Do think Dolores could read an email if it weren't for me? Janine is useless, but we get paid the same. I am off for one week in the summer, that's all. And half the time Sister Paul has me helping that drunk, Sal, like I am a janitor."

"Your shoulder is fine," I said, interrupting her tirade. Bernadette looked up in surprise. I was heartened to know that some synapses in my brain were firing.

"That is what you traded Tim for. He knew there was nothing wrong with your shoulder, but he told your doctor there was. And more importantly, he didn't tell anyone at school you were fine. So you could leave early and get all those student helpers."

Bernadette's ailment had been behind the creation of our 'work for detention' policy. Still, I could understand her frustration. It seemed that a school environment bred an absurdly lopsided division of labor, with those of lowest status responsible for the most work. But Bernadette's cure was worse than the disease.

"You should tell Sister Paul what you've done, Bernadette." I dropped the last gift bag from my hands, and turned it round. I did not want to look at our school motto, *Veritas vos liberabit.* The truths I was learning were not make me feel free at all.

"Why should I tell anybody anything? Nobody listens. You think everything in this school is so sacred? How come nobody cares when Dolores fits half the football team into schedules with the easiest teachers? Why does Sister let Sal work here, with all the times he has been in rehab? And that lecher, Ken Telford? Toni Anne isn't the only idiot who has fallen for his nonsense. Ask Sister Paul why he leaves every school that hires him."

She smacked her lips shut and shook her head.

"I've always known things nobody cared about until now, and I am not going to say another word." She looked at me defiantly and I felt suddenly ill. Bernadette no doubt had knowledge of so much hypocrisy, so many things that were not what they were supposed to be. And what should she have done with that information? I know I had long since dismissed her as a cantankerous crank, and was not as kind as I should have been. It didn't excuse her actions at all, but I felt sick for her anyway.

"You had better open your eyes, Addra." She warned me, fixing the tissue paper in her gift bag with expert ease. "Or you're going to get burned."

Chapter 10

"How many cookies may we take, Ms. Lake?" Little Seth, already had three in his hand, and seemed concerned he had transgressed.

"As many as you want, Seth." I answered warmly. "The only rule is not to leave me with any. I ate enough while making them."

It was true. My conversation with Bernadette had ruined another night of rest, one which I had desperately needed. Never reaching beyond a state of half sleep, thoughts fired through my brain like missiles, making it impossible to relax.

The only solution I could think of was to rise at 4:40 and bake cookies. This was technically the first Friday of the school year, since the last had been missed through tragedy, and I thought it appropriate to begin a new tradition. Whether apt or not, I thought of my little freshmen as young chicks, and wanted to shield them from harmful knowledge, like their mother hen. That I thought to keep them safe with chocolate chips spoke to my state of mind as did the clear association I felt with them. Despite my years, I felt strangely unprotected against the world around me, with small legs that would not carry me far from the would-be predators.

I was reaching for a cookie when Noah walked in.

"Hi, Mr. Stabler. Class, this is Mr. Stabler. He will be teaching you physics when you are juniors."

I smiled at both Noah and at Seth Tunstill, who was pulling out his small notebook.

"What's up?" I asked Noah.

"Sister Paul sent me," he began, "I am to take over your homeroom this morning. She wants to meet with you." Noah schooled his expression to neutrality, since the entire front row of my class was watching us, but I could see concern in his eyes.

I handed my cookie to Noah, and unlocked my bottom desk drawer to retrieve the Honors Program folder. I was fairly certain I would need it.

"Class, Mr. Stabler is going to stay and enjoy the cookies with you. If I am not back before the bell rings, have a wonderful weekend. Make sure you think about what we should have for Cookie Day, next week."

I had already dutifully gathered information on allergies and preferences, and was happy to find I would be dealing with nothing more concerning than the girls who wanted their cookies to be magically low fat while still retaining all their butter and sugar.

Noah spared a wink when he handed me my key card, which I had to return and retrieve.

On my way towards the exit, I saw Ginny look up when I passed her classroom. She did not seem surprised to find me out of mine. I filed that tidbit away as I walked out into the morning air. The Towers were quiet when I entered. I padded my way up to the carpeted second floor, expecting Jeremy Wrobleski to waylay me at any point. Only Janine was in the outer office and Bernadette's desk was empty.

I nodded at her before heading towards Sister Paul's office, annoyed with myself for being nervous.

"Addra, come in." Sister beckoned me from the other side of her closed door, which I, in turn, opened. I did not concern myself with how she knew it was me. When I entered my eyes fell to the two large computer screens that now sat upon her desk. Obviously my arrival had been observed.

I walked towards the chair I had sat in a week before and arranged myself in it before handing the Honors folder over.

"Ginny has graciously volunteered to help with administrative matters while we search for a new secretary."

I nodded, content to have one mystery solved. I also knew that Sister would say nothing more directly about Bernadette. I mentally tried to ready myself for the conversation to come. Sister wove her words in a subtle but complex tapestry; I knew to never speak without first measuring my own.

"The issue with this," she nodded towards the folder, "is a seismic one."

I fought through my nerves to process her statement. Bernadette was fired, Laurie Boone may not return to school, and Tim was dead.

"The other four students," I said.

Sister nodded. "Precisely. Their parents arranged with Mr. Boone to have their grades altered and their programs changed."

I knew Sister Paul was not asking me how she should handle this issue, that decision would be her own. So what was she telling me?

"The students should not be punished for the transgressions of their parents. But neither can they continue in the program."

Here Sister paused again, but I was unsure of how to respond, given that she had not asked me a question. I wondered if, for some reason, she was seeking my approval.

"There are other things, other things that have come to my attention."

My mind returned to the secrets Bernadette had enumerated for me last night. I wondered if she had opted not to remain quiet after all. Then there was the issue of Coach Brown accepting gifts from parents. Sister had been ignorant of much, it seemed.

"Once these matters are settled, Addra, I would like you to helm a true overhaul of the Honors Program. We need a system in place wherein we are aware of what occurs within those classes, to differentiate them from the others."

"I would be glad to Sister Paul."

"And please extend an invitation to Mr. Stabler to help, as he has already done."

I might have detected a small smile but with Sister Paul, they tended to disappear before you could confirm their initial presence.

"The truth will out, Addra. I do not wish you to worry about that."

"Yes, Sister."

155

I was more confirming her words rather than agreeing to their accuracy. So many truths had remained undiscovered until Tim's murder and there were doubtless more things Sister did not know.

"I feel I have failed, Addra, in trusting where I should not have trusted."

I heard the faint ringing of the bell, signaling the end of homeroom. I needed to go.

"We are all guilty of that, Sister Paul." I said before leaving. Like Bernadette had warned, we all needed to keep our eyes open.

I turned back to peer up at Jeremy Wrobleski's window before re entering my day.

"You coming to the game tomorrow, Ms. Lake?" Frankie was pushing all the desks in my room to one side, as Sal typically washed the floors over the weekend. I was adjusting the windows and their shades.

"Of course I am," I said with false enthusiasm, which I trusted would become authentic by tomorrow. At the moment my fatigue threatened to send me slumping to the floor in a sad heap.

I had already told Frankie there was nothing for him to carry to my car, because I could not imagine lifting my pen to grade all weekend. But I probably would have taken him up on an offer to carry me out, had he thought to ask.

Noah walked in to my room.

"Hey, Mr. Stabler, are you coming to the game?" At some point, Noah and Frankie had grown more comfortable with each other, which I was glad to see.

"I'm looking forward to it, Frankie. Ms. Lake?" He looked towards me.

"I never miss a game."

Excepting those early months after my accident, when I could not walk, I had never missed a game. My heart always clenched at how excited the athletes were to have you watch them play. It always brought me out, whether I really felt like it or not.

156

I thought back to when Frankie was in my 9th grade class. He had been sullen and unreachable until I had spoken to him about an impressive block he had made in the previous game. Thereafter he became my champion of sorts and we maintained a relationship which allowed him to demonstrate some budding chivalry while I was able to temper his dislike for school by showing him just how clever he really was.

"Saint Stanislaus has some brutes on their line." I said. "You play smart, Frankie."

"No worries, Ms. Lake." Frankie walked out of my classroom, already undoing his tie as he left.

Noah was smiling at me, softly.

"What?" I asked.

"You really love these kids, don't you?"

"Yes," I answered. "Some of them just crawl into my heart and don't leave." Frankie's initial belligerence was because of his stutter and fear of reading aloud. I had hated to think anyone would mock him for it.

"Do you want to go to the game with me?" I asked. I felt more at peace since my stilted conversation with Sister Paul. It was strangely comforting to know that someone above me in station and experience had been similarly in the dark about so many things. I trusted that Sister would learn from her omissions and move on.

"I would love to. We could make a whole day of it?" Noah asked.

I hesitated, but having been brave enough to ask him, I should be brave enough to tell him the full truth.

'Sitting in those bleachers usually does me in. I am not good for much besides hanging out on the couch after."

"That sounds perfect to me."

We walked to our cars together, hands almost touching.

When I awoke, early on Saturday morning, it was from a long, unbroken slumber. I was further gratified to

157

see the sun was going to shine, knowing how worse my leg would feel under a cloudy sky.

Since Noah wouldn't be picking me up until noon, I had plenty of time to do my stretching exercises, and take a long walk. I even sorted out my laundry when I came home, before showering and dressing in a carefully casual way.

Noah found me sitting out on my porch, with a tiny cooler filled with sandwiches I had made from the left over scones.

"Ham and cheese," I said, when he joined me on the porch. I said it quickly, before he could get in his own, slightly nonsensical greeting. He kissed me before saying anything at all.

"Did you sleep?"

"I did. I feel better knowing that Sister Paul is learning about all the things that have been going on behind her back."

Noah nodded. I had already told him last night about my fraught conversation with Bernadette and my less emotional one with Sister.

I wondered briefly how Bernadette felt when she woke up this morning. She always went to our football games, wearing an enormous school sweatshirt.

"Do you think Sister is going to do anything about Dolores?" Noah asked, thankfully interrupting my musing, which had threatened to become maudlin.

"Because Bernadette thought she gave preferential treatment to some athletes? I'm not sure. I wonder which teachers she thought were the easy ones."

More to the point, I was hoping I was not on that list. I doubted it, imagining that Mark's classes were more likely to be filled with a plethora of academically challenged, sport playing kids.

"Some of the juniors talked about her. They said she and Nick Morrison used to date in college."

The students must have heard that from Morrison, as I could not imagine Dolores saying anything that might suggest her age.

"Really?" I asked, slightly surprised. I always thought of Nick as being elderly, more so because of his limp, I imagined now, than anything else. I don't think I would have assumed he and Dolores to be that close in age.

I looked down at my cane, which I used to compensate for my own limp.

"I hate how judgmental I can be." I turned to Noah, hoping I would not need to explain myself more.

"Everybody does it sometimes Addra. At least you are aware of it and try to do it less. I see you and you have a terrible poker face."

I laughed, recalling how Noah paid attention.

"I was just so grateful, after my accident, that I had lived. I wanted to give something back, to honor God, but I don't feel like I am doing a very good job."

"Then you don't see what I see." Noah gave me another kiss before his eyes grew serious, behind his glasses.

"May I ask what happened?"

I knew he was asking about that accident. Anyone who ever asked me about it, avoided calling it anything when they did.

"I had kept my car home and walked that day, with some thought about working off all the calories I was consuming that week."

Yesterday's baking was hardly novel. I practically tried a new cookie recipe for every day between Thanksgiving and Christmas.

"I stayed late at school to get all my research papers graded so I would be free for the holiday. It was after seven when I was walking home, the kids had already gone home from football practice."

I did recall thinking how quiet the campus had seemed. It had damp and foggy too. But I had felt no sense of foreboding which bothered me now.

"I went out the alley behind the athletic fields, and was walking around the 10th avenue cul de sac when a car hit me."

"You were on the sidewalk?" Noah asked.

"Yes, but I am not even sure from what direction I was hit. I just remember feeling the head lights on me and then the impact. I was thrown against some trees and knocked unconscious. One of the homeowners, Mr. Delgado, found me, but the car was long gone."

I didn't feel like talking about my recovery, or all of the scars are bore from the tree branches I hit, or the blood I lost from the compound fractures in my right leg. I told Noah the story of Mr. Delgado and his dog-crap catching camera instead.

We laughed for a bit before I added,

"There's more, I just don't feel like talking about it now."

Noah offered me his hand and grasped the cooler in the other one.

"We have plenty of time," he answered.

I told Noah to pull into the regular lot, off of Mayflower Road. Our key cards would give us access and we would be able to make a faster get away at the end of the game here, than from the crowded spectator lot on the other side of the football field.

"Smart lady," he said, as we pulled up beside other cars, all with the St. Augustine's parking pass hanging from their rear view mirrors.

Nick Morrison was getting out of his own car as we did.

"Is this new?" I asked him, recalling that he had driven a small, two door sports model last year, and not this silver sedan.

"Relatively new," he answered. "It's easier to get in and out of."

Thinking about my own, oddly shaped Beetle, I could see his point. Nick had limped for as long as I had known him, but had never spoke about it.

"This is going to be your first game, Stabler?"

Nick and Noah began to chat, while I thought some more about the Athletic Director. He was always affable when I saw him and grateful for the carefully worded recommendation letters I wrote for many of the athletes, but I had had little reason to interact with him.

Considering the location of his office and his need to be here whenever a practice or a game was taking place, he must have dealt with Tim Boone on a regular basis. I wondered again why I had never seen him at physical therapy but concluded that he could have traveled to Binghamton for treatment. Not everyone was comfortable with how painfully intertwined things could be in Moreland.

"Do you think the guys will be alright today, Nick? I know the police have been asking Coach a lot of questions."

Noah just peered at me, indicating that I had changed their conversational topic with little finesse.

"Those detectives have definitely been a distraction and Coach has been meeting with Sister Paul a lot too. Mike Brown is a good guy." He said this with more vehemence that I had ever observed from him before.

"He can be a little sloppy but he is a great coach and a great motivator. I just wish I had been there that morning. I would have known if the door was locked."

I chose not to give any indication that I knew what he was talking about.

"Well, hopefully it will all be over soon, like Sister said at Parent Information Night." Noah's addition had the sound of a closing comment.

Nick took the hint and said that he was off to the Towers, to escort Sister Paul down to the game. The woman did love her processionals, I thought, once again, unkindly.

I wanted to continue to think about Nick Morrison, especially when I saw Sal glaring at him, from across the parking lot. Unfortunately, seeing Sal outside the athletic building, with a black garbage bag once again in his hand, was too much of a shock for me. I stumbled, causing Noah to drop the cooler and catch me.

By the time I straightened myself up and explained that I was fine, Sal was gone. But I had my answer to at least one more question that had been troubling me. It had been Sal hiding in the trees behind

161

me, on Thursday night. I knew it, because I had finally recalled that the voice had whispered the very same thing Sal had said to me the day we found Tim's body. "He was already here."

Sal was trying to tell me something, only he was unwilling to do so directly. I knew approaching him now would serve no purpose. I needed to think about this when I had the time. As we neared the stands, the smells of coffee, popcorn, and boiled hotdogs mingled, less divisively than one might think.

Music was already blasting from the loud speaker and most of the seats had been filled. Noah and I went up to the rows reserved for faculty. His solicitude, I assumed, would be explainable by my condition. Ginny eyed us as we sat.

"Those Stanislaus boys are big." Noah said, emphasizing the last word. I nodded, and concentrated on nothing more but the game and the feel of Noah sitting close beside me.

It took an unsurprising amount of effort, and a last minute stop of the Stanislaus offence for the game to end with our victory. My voice was hoarse from yelling encouragement at Frankie and the rest of our defensive line. I whispered to Noah that we should go, before the inevitable announcements about raffle winners and booster club sales could begin.

As expected, the hours sitting on a hard bench seat made me appear as elderly and crooked as Nick Morrison when I walked but my cane also cleared a nice path for us. I nodded to Ginny's hand gesture that I was to call her later.

"I guess the story is out now." Noah announced, nodding in her direction. When we rounded the field and began to walk back towards the parking lot, he took my hand.

"Do you care?" He asked.

"Nope," I answered, and proved my veracity by continuing to hold on to his hand as someone ran up behind us, calling my name.

"Brian," I exclaimed, surprised.

I had never actually seen Brian out and about, away from the therapy office and the Big Bean. He was wearing the hooded sweatshirt of our opponent and I took him for a St. Stanislaus alum.

"Hey, Addra. Noah." He put his hands on his knees and took a few, hard breathes.

"I was on the other end of the field," he wheezed, "when I saw you get up and leave."

I waited for him to tell us what had been important enough for him to break into an impromptu sprint. Immediately concerned for his repaired knee, I was about to inquire after it when he said,

"Audrey just texted me that Dougie got arrested."

"You're kidding." I answered, before turning to Noah and muttering, "Angry Cop."

"Did they get him for the dealing or for Tim's murder?"

"Or both," Noah said quietly.

"Not sure, man, but it is crazy. Audrey is pretty upset. I'm going over to her place now."

I smiled at Brian, who did not look similarly upset, but even had some nice color, from his run in the chill or from thoughts of comforting Audrey. Either way, I was glad for his news and told him so.

"Come by the Bean tomorrow."He gave me a companionable nudge before galloping off. I had forgotten the other day, when thanking God for my new friends, to include Brian, but I amended that now.

"So it might be over," Noah, began, as he let me into his car, waving at someone when he closed the door.

I peered up to get a glance at Sal, once again visible in the distance. I did not think it was over yet but kept my thoughts to myself.

Chapter Eleven

"It is incumbent upon all of us to raise as much as possible in our fundraising efforts," Dolores continued, in her whispery tone.

The entire faculty, save once again for Ken Telford, was meeting in the same cerulean colored conference room, as on our first Monday, two weeks prior. Before Noah went home last night, he had presciently reminded me of this early morning gathering.

Now I could vaguely recall shoving the memo, festooned with pumpkins and brightly hued leaves, into my bag, from whence it had stayed, unread.

Before I could catch myself, I smiled, preferring to think about the weekend I had just spent, than the Fall Festival and Fundraiser. I was sure to soon despise that alliterative jumble of a day, once Dolores finished reminding me what it was.

Noah had made good on his promise to enjoy a Saturday spent propped up amongst the pillows of my sofa. We had each chosen movies to watch and had flipped a coin to determine if Paolo's Pizza Palace or the Golden Noodle would deliver our dinner. Saturday had also run naturally into Sunday, as Noah fell asleep upon said sofa in the midst of my chosen classic, *Now, Voyager*.

I had watched the movie until it's ending, and then dragged myself off to sleep, checking the locks for good measure. My house was small enough that I fell asleep listening to Noah's own breathing down the hall. Our Sunday was not nearly as lazy. Having Noah accompany me on my walk was so much more enjoyable we had covered twice as much distance as I typically did. We talked easily and I gave less thought than usual to the cars that passed us.

I found being with him comfortable, yet exciting at the same time. It was a happy melding. I was not a particularly dramatic person, so in my younger years had been drawn to men who were high strung and given to demanding more than they gave. Noah attracted me specifically because he was not like that. His self possession was intriguing and his quiet nature matched my own.

Besides awakening this morning grateful for Noah, I also had occasion to be thankful that my absence from school last June, had, at the very least, kept me from being drawn into the Fall Festival and Fundraiser executive committee. Just thinking of that experience threatened to wipe away all of the restful rejuvenation I had gained over the weekend.

In yet another strange mimicry of our initial Labor Day meeting, assignments were distributed and frantically read. Opening the black and gold embossed folder, I was immediately struck by how many funds Sister would save if she would just use generic manila envelopes, like countless other organizations did. As it was, I maintained a pile of these school folders that my frugal soul struggled to find uses for.

In recognition of my condition, my job was that of 'pie lady.' Essentially I was to procure volunteers to bake and donate pies that I would then lure visitors to the festival into buying. I could easily imagine baking most of the delicacies myself, as I was inordinately proud of my pie crust. Ginny, who was on the executive committee, must have recalled my boasting and chosen to put it to good use.

I glanced over the sheet to discover Noah would be a part of a blacksmithing guild, with the remaining men of science. I spent a moment picturing that, my day dream nicely focused on his forearms as they wielded a heavy hammer to strike a newly formed tool.

Returning to my reading, I noted the history department would be using period authentic tools to churn butter and make maple candy, as was befitting a landscape that had once allowed the monks to live self sufficiently.

There would also be offerings of face painting, apple bobbing, craft making, as well as the requisite raffle items. The students, it seemed, were being enjoined to sell staggering amounts of these raffle tickets to the Moreland community.

165

As Dolores explained it, the parents had already been informed that their help was required in the form of ticket buying, booth sponsorship, and raffle item donations. The level of parental contribution was to be determined by how many children they had enrolled in the school, as well as what clubs and sports their children belonged too.

The complexity of the operation made me wonder if Bernadette was missed. She had always been in charge of the myriad lists and tallies required for such monumental fundraising events.

"Nick," Dolores continued, "we are counting on the contributions of the scholar athletes, as we have in the past."

Nick Morrison nodded at Dolores, but even I could see that his smile was tight.

"Maybe Sister should have waited to clamp down on Brown," someone whispered behind me.

It was true that the coach had always outfitted past fundraising effort with vital items. We sold the cases of water and soda his boys carried in. At our last walk-a-thon we had all worn tee shirts Coach Brown said were a gift from the team. Like many, I had not given this generosity much thought or appreciation.

Despite knowing that his contributions were made through his own 'horse trading' with parents, I felt slightly ashamed. The administration certainly put pressure on the athletic staff to raise substantial sums of money. Like Bernadette, Coach Brown's methods were wrong but I could not judge him beyond that. We were always being told that our future was held by the same thread tethering this school to its own existence. And it was our responsibility to ensure the school did not fall.

Judging from Dolores' further comments, each teacher was to secure student volunteers to help set up the booths on Friday and to dismantle them after the actual fundraiser on Saturday. To facilitate this we were going to have a half day on Friday.

Sighing slightly, I made a mental note to plan quizzes for that day. The prospect of early dismissal, especially on a Friday, could turn even the most docile student into a demon. I had long ago opted for testing as an alternative to the mind numbing headache I would otherwise have before the early dismissal bell rang.

By the curious magic of scheduling, early dismissal days began with an extra long homeroom period, and I spent some more minutes ignoring Dolores' speech, in favor of deciding what special treat I would be baking for my homeroom. To wit, I almost missed her final comments and started when I heard her say,

"Though I do not put much stock in rumors, I have heard that plans are already in motion for some students to vandalize our efforts, after we have set up the Fall Festival booths. I hope that this is not case but please, everyone, do you best to council your students against such sabotage. These actions would be amoral as well as foolhardy, given our new security systems. But students, especially seniors, enjoy their pranks without thought to the consequences."

I watched her look in Nick Morrison's direction again, though she could also have been directing her attention to Coach Brown, who was seated next to him. The football team had been responsible for a few pranks in the past, usually around Homecoming time. But Dolores had employed the stronger term, vandalism, which I could not see them committing. I spent a moment enjoying the irony of Dolores' claim that she put little stock in rumors, until Sister Paul rose to speak.

She did not address anything that Dolores had just said, but instead announced,

"The police have informed me that they had arrested a suspect in the murder of Mr. Boone and that this man is in no way connected to St. Augustine's. I am sure this fact will be well broadcasted by the media but I wanted to be the first to inform you."

I turned in my chair, to find Noah. Angry Cop, I thought to myself, while assuming that he could hear me too.

After he nodded, I moved on to notice Mark waving at me. He indicated that I was to stay here after the meeting adjourned.

Ginny and Sister Paul also remained seated when we were dismissed and we all received curious glances as the other teachers filed out. I noticed Toni Anne walked out without looking back once but Noah managed a wink that I believe only I caught.

Without preamble, Sister announced, "Ken Telford is no longer an employee here. Mark and I are already exploring alternatives, but for the now, Miriam Dulskie will be rejoining our staff tomorrow." She had named the retired teacher who had taken my place last semester.

"The students, if they should ask, need only be told that Mr. Telford had a family emergency. The newspaper will be on hiatus until his permanent replacement is found." Sister rose and exited without another word.

"What else could we tell the kids? We don't know anything, do we, Mark?"

Ginny looked angrily at our chairperson. Ken's leaving did not really affect her but she was miffed not to be let in on whatever secret had spirited him away.

Mark looked incredulous.

"Sister Paul sent me an email last night, telling me essentially the same thing. I have no idea what is going on."

I shrugged when Ginny turned toward me.

"I know Addra," she snickered. "You are so out of the loop, you cannot even see it from where you sit."

It was not until Tim's murder was solved that I realized how unnerved I had been on campus. My sense of relaxation was palpable now, though I was consciously sweeping my thoughts about Sal Vacarro aside. I spent my lunch period in my classroom, arranging for my Friday quizzes and alphabetizing my collected assignments. I had already called Audrey to cancel my afternoon therapy appointment and intended to stay at school until all my papers were graded. Self imposed deadlines were necessary for me to keep apace of the amount of work I assigned. Nothing would goad a person into effort better than the specter of twenty five angry teenagers, who had been promised their grades back and were not getting them.

Johnny Marchiano stopped by at the end of the day. Since I planned on bringing nothing home later, I drafted him into window duty, while I patrolled the room for trash.

"You heard about the cop?" His question confirmed that Angry Cop had been the one arrested for Tim's murder. I hoped that he learned this in discussion with Laurie, since she and her mother should be told of breaks in the case before anyone else.

"How is Laurie doing?"

"She hasn't wanted to see me much, Ms. Lake. But I took your advice and have been really patient and she said I could stop by this afternoon. Practice is voluntary so I already told Coach I was skipping it and going to Laurie's."

I peered at the young man a moment. Since boys his age hid their emotions with less finesse than the girls, I detected disappointment in his tone.

His feelings for Laurie were already clear so I asked,

"Has Coach been riding you?"

I expected so, and was saddened when he nodded. It was of paramount importance, to me at least, that students see only our professional best, and not our private troubles.

"This stuff with Mr. Boone really had him rattled. And now we have this fu---"

He stopped and smiled at me sheepishly before continuing. I understood immediately, since that particular alliterative word fit my feelings for the Fall Festival and Fundraiser equally well.

"We have all this fundraising to do, way more than any other kids. Mr. Morrison has really been laying the pressure on us. You have to sell a hundred tickets per sport, even when you are on a spring sport."

I recalled that Johnny played second base for our baseball team in the spring and shook my head in sympathy. Here was a different form of 'trickle down' economics, where the adults need for funding was brought to the children to solve.

"He is out of control," Johnny added.

"Coach Brown?"

"Nah, Mr. Morrison. He used to be pretty cool and stay out of the way. But ever since last year he is always flipping out about something. Even Mr. Boone didn't like him."

"People handle stress differently, Johnny. Mr. Morrison has a lot to deal with." I was thinking of his persistent limp, which I expected also came with great pain. I was quite conscious of the effect that pain could have on one's outlook.

Johnny looked down at my leg for a moment, and I watched him, gladdened that he was processing my intimations on his own. If I could teach my kids anything before they graduated it would be that life was never simple. It could be wonderful and unexpected at times, but it was never simple.

"I get it, Ms. Lake. You know, I am taking Laurie somewhere really nice tonight."

He moved towards the doorway and said over his shoulder.

"You should have Mr. Stabler take you somewhere nice too."

Johnny was most likely already on his date by the time I found my voice.

At a few minutes past five I had had enough. A well placed jacket underneath my propped leg mitigated any pain, but the rumblings in my stomach were becoming ominous. My metabolism demanded a pretty steady stream of food and I had denied it for just long enough. I was still on the right side of crankiness, but I needed to get home.

Since we were still some weeks away from the end of Daylight Savings Time, a bit of light remained to guide my way. A sizable number of players had opted to attend the voluntary practice, judging from the noise I heard walking past the football field. I spared a prayer for Johnny and Laurie. My own romantic past made me no expert on relationships but I hoped that they could be good for each other, for however long it lasted. My own parents had been together since high school, and I couldn't imagine anything working out better.

Naturally my thoughts turned to Noah and I only turned them away through effort. I was nearing the alley way and needed to be attentive. I noticed some cigarette butts had returned. Was it impossible to sustain change? Sometimes I wondered how much my accident had changed me. I could not decide if it would be better or worse to have gone through all this unaltered.

Wanda and Mitch were at their accustomed posts when I exited the alley and I put my philosophical musings aside, with ease.

As I approached their stoop I noticed they were both chewing, in addition to puffing on their cigarettes. I sighed with relief.

"I candy my own pecans," Wanda said, offering me the bowl. I took her offering literally and sat down with the bowl in my lap, propping my cane against their railing.

"How are you guys? I haven't seen you in a while."

Mitch grinned.

"Yeah? Well, we've seen you, kid."

His wife nudged him before answering.

"Now that school has started, our daughter needs us for more babysitting duty. But we did see you Sunday morning, with a very nice looking young man."

She gave me a sidelong glance. It sat so strangely upon her grandmotherly countenance that I laughed.

171

"He's a friend from school. His name is Noah. I like him."

"Told you," Wanda said to Mitch. "A woman can always tell."

I chewed on that comment along with my pecans, letting them change the course of the conversation.

"Five sets of St. Augustine kids have already come asking us to buy Festival tickets and raffle tickets." Mitch said

"Already?" I asked, since it was only Monday. "Maybe you should keep your tickets in your pocket, as proof that you have already bought enough."

I knew Mitch and Wanda were soft touches. They would be at the Festival when it opened and would have a chance to win every single prize we offered.

"It should be a lovely time, especially now," I hedged.

"Yup. It's great that Boone's murder was solved but I hate that another cop was responsible."

"Drugs," Wanda whispered, shaking her curly head.

I shook my head too and handed her back the now depleted.

"I have to get your recipe for those. I made a maple pumpkin pie that they would be the perfect topping for."

In fact, I was sure that when combined with the nuts, the pie would become the hit of the Festival. I'd be darned if I wasn't getting excited about the thing, only hours past my initial scorn. That was the perverse charm of St. Augustine's, it always pulled you in.

"Well, this has been a long day. I'll see you guys soon."

"Take care, Sweetie," they said, nearly in unison.

"Bring Noah by soon."

"We have definitely been found out," I told him a few hours later.

I was in my pajamas, ice cream bowl in hand, when I called him.

"Why? Because Brian gave me a man-hug when I saw him on Main Street?" Noah laughed.

"No, because my neighbors want to meet the 'nice looking man' they say me with on Sunday."

"Which one said I was nice looking, the husband or the wife?"

"And," I continued, ignoring him. "Johnny Marchiano suggested you take me out someplace good tonight."

"Did he? Does that mean I have the approval of your team? I have to tell you, Addra, those boys are crazy about you. I keep waiting for Frankie DiMeo to take me aside and explain what will happen to me if I get fresh with you."

I whooped a bit, having no trouble picturing the same.

"I try to give them the opportunity to be good." I said, explaining my relationship with many of my students.

"You are like that with everyone," Noah murmured.

"Not everyone. I could not like Ken Telford, but with good reason I suppose."

"Now, you won't have to." Noah responded, again confirming the power of the St. Augustine gossip chain.

"Do you think he was fired for the affair? Toni Anne still has her job."

"Toni Anne isn't the one who was married," I pointed out. "Though I think she is just as guilty, maybe Sister does not."

"But what they do in their private life shouldn't affect their jobs."

"We are employees at will, according to our contracts, and there is a morality clause buried deep within it." The private school world was a far cry from the union-backed public school system that Noah was accustomed to.

173

"I hope it doesn't violate the morality clause to say that I miss you."

"It doesn't. And I might quit if it did."

Chapter Twelve

"You know, Addra, those boys are out of control."

I was standing with Mr. Delgado. He had his rake in one hand while I held my cane with both of mine. He had pulled me over from my walk, where typically a wave sufficed.

"What boys?" I asked, knowing that he would likely say the football team. Mr. Delgado was often bothered by the noise they made.

"Those football hooligans. The noise last night! I heard music, and screaming, and all sorts of fuss and bother. Finally had to call the police. They came right away."

I did not understand him.

"You heard their sirens?"

"No, I walked through the alley, and a bit up towards the fields. It isn't trespassing," he pointed out. "That limping guy does it."

Since I assumed Mr. Delgado was referring to Nick Morrison, who must walk to school sometimes, the situations were not analogous. Ignoring that, I asked

"Did you see them arrest anyone?"

"No, but I heard that fool of a coach yelling about liquor. Those kids must have gotten themselves drunk." Mr. Delgado began to rake again, with a spirit suggestive of his feelings for the demon liquor.

I was inclined to agree with him. I was also sick to think that the boys would make so foolish a choice, in light of the negative publicity the school had received. I was also naïve enough to be shocked that they could so easily obtain alcohol; some of the boys on the J.V. squad were just ninth and tenth graders.

After apologizing to Mr. Delgado, I turned toward home. As a representative of St. Augustine's and doubtless the teacher of some of those boys, I felt the burden of their folly. I was also aghast that Coach Brown would allow another security breach in the midst of the tumult from his first.

Anxious to get to school and see if I couldn't find some answers, I drove in, despite earlier plans to walk. I was sure today was going to prove a long one, despite not having yet begun.

"In criticism I will be bold, and as sternly, absolutely just with friend as foe. From this purpose nothing shall turn me."

I was reading these words to my sophomore class, but Edgar Allan Poe had written them. I thought it important the students know that Poe had been a respected literary critic, and not only a spinner of macabre tales. Thus far, the going was slowed by my constant correction of their errors while recounting his biography.

I was of two minds, when it came to teaching Poe. His gruesome stories did appeal to the teenaged love of horror and I was glad for any attention they gave. But so much of what they believed about Poe was wrong and I usually felt stymied by their lack of interest in the truth.

So I disabused them of the belief that he married his eleven year old sister, replacing it with a still troubling marriage to his thirteen year old cousin. I informed them that there was no evidence that Poe was a drug addict and more supposition than proof that he drank excessively.

It was true that he had died, after being found raving in the streets, wearing someone else's clothing. But no definitive answer to the cause of his demise has ever been found. Except, I told them firmly, he was not a vampire. I had already grown tired of their recent obsession with vampires.

"So what was wrong with him?"

"It is difficult to say, given the limitations to medical knowledge in the nineteenth century," I began before being interrupted by the same student.

"I heard he had rabies."

A few students made sounds of disgust.

"That was one theory, as was diabetes, heart failure, cholera, epilepsy. We will most likely never know, but can enjoy the perverse irony of a man some credit with creating the modern detective story, dying in such a mysterious way."

I looked around the room, to see if anyone was enjoying the irony, but mostly saw frustrated, somewhat bored expressions. In my experience, most teenagers wanted answers, and they were deeply distrustful of topics that were not so easily put to rest.

I was about to make a pun about how many of Poe's characters were not so easily put to rest, even after dying, but knew I would be the only one to laugh. We needed to read a few of his poems and short stories before my humor had a chance of being appreciated. I usually saved *The Raven* for Halloween, but would be periodically returning to his short stories throughout the fall.

First, I wanted to return to the idea of literary criticism, in an attempt to turn them from writing 'a book report' when I asked them to analyze a literary work. This particular class relied too much on summarization. I had killed two red pens while grading their summer reading journals, fruitlessly searching for some attempt at analysis.

"Let us look at this quotation again." I pointed to the board. "How to Poe view his role as a critic?"

"He took it seriously," someone offered.

"He thought he should criticize his friends and enemies the same way," Josie, a girl who had fought not to sit in the front row, answered.

"Yes," I agreed. "When doing his work Poe believed himself duty bound to fairly assess what he read, without regard to whether the author was his friend or not. Should we admire his stance?"

I was asking only for good measure, not expecting anyone to argue against a regard for fairness. So I was surprised when one boy, Fred, called out,

"What kind of a friend was he? You should take care of your friends."

A few of the girls rolled their eyes, as they were accustomed to doing when anyone spoke, including me. But a few others nodded, in response to Fred's assertion.

Belatedly I recalled he was on the football team, and regretted not scraping this entire lesson before I began it.

Five boys, all seniors and juniors, had been suspended for their role in procuring liquor and getting drunk from it after practice last night. When the police arrived, they had found many of the team horsing around, but the majority of them did so soberly. Coach had been in the athletic office, with the door closed, and was not aware of what had transpired until the police officer came to get him. The parents of those five boys had to come to school to retrieve them, as a few had driven themselves to school that day.

I had heard that much from Ginny, who had sources in various places around the school. But she had not been sure which students had been suspended nor what punishment would be meted out to all the players, who had collectively refused to say where the liquor came from. For now, the rest of those present last night were attending classes, but it made it difficult to keep focused on the lesson.

"We should all take care of our friends, certainly. But lying either to them or for them is not taking care of them." I made this point while looking around the room at each student, before bringing my comment back around to Poe.

"Wouldn't Poe be a better friend to another writer if he honestly assessed his work and told him where it was flawed?"

'But aren't you being a better friend if you protect the other person from being criticized?" Josie asked.

"Yeah," this comment found support from Fred. "You have to look out for your friends. Some of you do it."

He looked at me accusingly and continued before I could stop him.

"Mrs. Donovan takes care of Mr. Morrison. Coach says she got him this job."

A few students looked to me to confirm this, which I had no intention of doing, even if I knew for sure. I had heard a few times that Dolores and Nick

Morrison were longtime friends and supposed Coach Brown was the one spreading the information around. What else did he tell the team about his colleagues?

"There is an important difference between helping and enabling, Fred. Now we have strayed from our original topic, but why don't you all create a vocabulary web for homework tonight, using the word enable."

I reminded them that this assignment would be posted on the class web page just before the bell rang. I smiled at the class as they existed, but felt curiously dissatisfied. Judging from their expressions, they felt the same.

It was inevitable that I later dreamt of Poe. He was not wandering the streets of Baltimore, but the St. Augustine campus. He emerged from the alley way, putting his hand forward to steady himself. In my dream I followed him, the wet leaves causing me to lurch forward too. I watched him limp from tree to tree, tugging at his ill-fitting clothes.

He was winding his way to the athletic building, whose door stood wide. Tim was there, half in the shadow and half in the light from the doorway. He was raising his hand to pull Poe towards him, when I woke up.

I did not sleep again, worried that the detectives had made a mistake, and Tim's murderer still walked free.

Frankie DiMeo arrived at my door, Wednesday afternoon, flexing his hands. He looked ready to shred my canvas bag, with all the books still inside it. I was glad to have hidden it away in my desk.

Like Johnny, Frankie had demurred from the optional practice Monday night, preferring to work out with his dad. He had already regaled me with tales of how much his father could bench press, and was hopeful to still be so strong when "he got old."

179

But Sister Paul continued to apply pressure to the entire team, in her effort to discover where the alcohol had come from. I offered no opinions about either her actions or the uniform silence of the players but was worried about everyone involved. I imagined this partly accounted for Frankie's initial look of consternation.

"No bags, Ms. Lake?"

"Nope, heading out to physical therapy. And I wanted to give my classes a break."

My surprise quizzes were copied and set to go for our early dismissal day Friday.

Frankie suddenly laughed, which made me glad.

"Are you giving your surprise quizzes on Friday?"

I stared at him, flabbergasted and no longer as pleased. Had someone seen me carrying the copies back to my classroom? Did my key card not work properly and students were riffling through my desk drawers while I was away?

"Ms. Lake, Ms. Lake," Frankie called to me loudly, breaking me from a reverie that had me in Sister Paul's office, demanding to look at surveillance tapes.

"You gave a surprise quiz every time we had a half day. It wasn't all that surprising after the first time."

I stared at him for another moment more, before beginning to laugh so hard I snorted. Luckily Frankie was affable enough to laugh with me and say nothing about my piggish noises.

"You didn't think we knew?"

"Well," I began, "you always looked surprised."

"Nobody wanted to hurt your feelings, Ms. Lake."

I found that extremely amusing too and continued to laugh, just this short of hysterically.

'I'm sorry, Frankie." I wiped tears away from my eyes.

"No problem, Ms. Lake. My mom finds weird things funny too."

Digesting that, I led him out of the room, pulling the door firmly behind me.

"No offense, but teachers think students never notice anything. We do, you know? We just don't always pay attention."

I followed him down the stairs, promising to mend my ways. Too many times I had been surprised by my own inattentiveness. It needed to stop.

To put a fine point on this self assessment, I swore and went back up the stairs. This time I had my key card with me but not the keys to my own house.

By the time I had entered my classroom and failed to be soothed by my lavender, I decided to skip physical therapy and go home. I just wasn't thinking straight and Frankie's comment, that we noticed things without paying attention to them, was gnawing at the corners of my mind. It intensified when Audrey informed me that Angry Cop had been released.

"Oh, Dougie is in big trouble for the weight loss pills," she added. "But he has an alibi for Tim's murder."

"Why did it take this long for an alibi?"

I chose to be angry at Angry Cop, for the return of my feeling of menace. And how must Laurie Boone and her mother feel now?

"He was with a lady," Audrey whispered. "A married lady."

"Doesn't anybody honor their marriage vows?" I asked priggishly, while furiously thinking of what I should do next. Angry Cop's release would surely be in the news, and I hoped that Detective Lawson would inform Sister Paul that we were right back where we started, almost two weeks ago.

No, I corrected myself, while telling Audrey goodbye. We were not as we had been two weeks ago, things had changed. Ken Telford was gone, his affair discovered. Coach Brown no longer used his players to gain favors from their parents. The grades that Bernadette had altered were fixed and the students back in the courses best suited to their abilities.

But I still felt the pull of the myriad rumors and guileless comments that I had heard since Tim died. Half formed thoughts had been whispering their knowledge to me, but I had not listened. Tim's murderer belonged to St. Augustine's and my feeling of dread returned, stronger and more constant than before.

I left the academic building as quickly as I could, clutching my house keys as a talisman. While walking out , I passed the security camera that was trained on the door.

Was Sister Paul looking into her computer screen at this very moment? Did my face betray the terror I suddenly felt? And what of the guilt? Clues had been dropping into my lap for days and I had done nothing about them but dream.

I began to walk across the lawn, and thought of Sal Vacarro. Twice he had told me, 'he was already here.' Both times I had assumed he meant Tim, but what if he had meant Tim's killer?

The police had just taken it for truth that only Sal, Scott Pearson, and I were on campus the morning Tim was murdered. Had they given any thought to the killer arriving on foot, and then stealing away after? He could have driven in later with the other faculty, feigning surprise at the news of what he knew had done.

Pieces of the puzzle, that I should have put together earlier, were falling into rapid place. My 10th street neighbors had all reported often seeing an old, limping man follow the alley way onto campus. I had also made the mistake of thinking Nick Morrison older than he was, because of that limp.

But what had I been told? He and Dolores were old friends, they had dated in college. She had gotten him this job and protected him in it. Why? Everyone else involved with Tim had been so through lies and knowledge they did not want shared with the world. What was Nick Morrison hiding?

As quickly as my cane could carry me, I walked down the alley, reviewing everything that I knew of Nick. Johnny Marchiano said that he was a changed man, not as affable as he had been before last year. Nick had told Coach Brown that Tim was a snake, while Tim reportedly had not liked Nick either.

182

Nick had replaced his sports car with a larger one, presumably because his injury was not one he believed would get better. He was always on campus, but ostensibly not on the occasions where it most counted like the morning Tim was killed or the night the boys brought liquor onto the football field.

I reached the cul de sac and stopped, staring at Mr. Delgado's neat house. More specifically, I stared at the poorly disguised camera that adorned Mr. Delgado's house.

Just like that, I realized what I had been missing. I was not the only one who cut through the alley to sneak onto campus. And just like I had been captured on film, I was betting the murderer had been as well.

It took Mr. Delgado only a few seconds to answer my frantic knock.

"Addra," he exclaimed, opening the screen door for me.

"What is the matter?"

"Mr. Delgado, have you gone through all your video evidence yet, for the pooper?"

"Why no," he said, as I slowly realized, we were not alone. Every light in the house appeared to be on so I easily saw a woman of Mr. Delgado's generation sitting on his plastic covered sofa. There was a tea service placed on the end table beside her. I had interrupted Mr. Delgado and his lady friend's date.

"Mr. Delgado, I am so sorry but I think the man who murdered Tim Boone,"

I paused while Mr. Delgado muttered, "hooligans."

"I think you might have captured him on your camera."

"Really?" he asked, looking momentarily nonplussed.

"Why Walter," his lady friend croaked from the sofa, "you're a hero."

Chapter 13

It took Mr. Delgado, Helen, and I little time to discover that I was correct. As carefully as he did everything else, Mr. Delgado had been taking his video tapes out of the recorder nightly, and labeling them by date. He intended there to be ample evidence for when the unrepentant dog walkers were finally caught.

My hands were shaking too much to place the video from early last Friday into the cassette player, but as Mr. Delgado did so, I rose from my seat, to move closer to the small screen.

Since the tapes recorded in twelve hour intervals, Mr. Delgado had programmed them to begin at six in the evening and end twelve hours later.

"I knew those hooligans would do their nasty work in the dark," he explained proudly.

We fast forwarded through some hours of nothingness, the camera trained to see from Mr. Delgado's walkway, the copse of trees to the left of his property, and the very corner of the alleyway. Randomly I thought that Mr. Delgado would have recorded my accident, had his camera been set up eight months earlier.

Shocking us all, a figure stepped into view, breaking up the darkness. But it was only a woman walking her leashed dog.

"That's Monica with little Pepper," Helen pointed out. I sensed that Mr. Delgado was disappointed when Monica did as she should with her little baggie.

We continued to watch as the nighttime hours shifted and soon, even the black and white footage seemed to register a change in shadow, as daylight approached. I felt my tension release, and be replaced by something much harder to define, as a new figure appeared at the corner of Mr. Delgado's property.

Nick walked slowly. His face was obscured by a hood, but the St. Augustine logo was clearly visible as he walked past Mr. Delgado's property. His limp gave him away regardless. None of us spoke for a moment, after watching him slip into the alleyway and out of view.

"So that was it?" Mr. Delgado sounded a bit nervous.

"That was it." I rose and gave him a hug. "Mr. Delgado I am going to have to call the police to come and get this tape, is that alright?"

"Sure, Addra, sure." He was rubbing his hands along the front of his pants. Even Helen seemed to think he was acting strangely.

"What is it, Walter?"

Mr. Delgado met my eyes, instead of hers.

"I see him a lot Addra. Walks off his benders, late at night, early in the morning. Didn't stop to think who he was."

"You saw him drunk?" I asked, understanding just whom the football boys and Coach were covering for.

"Yeah," he answered, but said no more.

I turned away to dial Detective Lawson's number, hoping he would pick up this time.

"I have nothing to say about this." Detective Lawson stepped out of Mr. Delgado's house and joined me on his stoop. I vaguely wondered if Wanda and Mitch were babysitting again, as their house was dark.

"Alright," I responded, not having intended to ask him any but one question.

"Will Nick be in school tomorrow?" I heard the catch in my own voice and was disappointed.

"No. You can go to work tomorrow. I know you will keep this quiet."

I looked up at the Detective, who had not sat down. This time, his statement held no suggestion of a question.

"Tell Mr. Delgado thank you for me?"

I didn't feel like going back into the house and had already phoned Noah to pick me up.

"I will." He left me on the outside, with no interview conducted. I had to believe that Lawson would learn everything he needed to from Nick Morrison and possibly, I added to myself, Dolores Donovan.

I walked out to the street, as Noah turned into the cul de sac, so I could be ready to meet him.

"What happened?" He asked as soon as I got into the car. When I called him, I had only whispered the address and all but begged him to come get me. I had calmed down somewhat in the interval.

I indicated Mr. Delgado's house behind me, reminding him of my story of the camera and the dog deposits.

"His camera recorded Nick Morrison walking into the alley, early on the morning Tim was killed."

I watched Noah's eyes widen behind his glasses.

"What did Tim have over Nick?" He asked me, cutting to the heart of the matter.

I thought about the car marks along the wall of the alleyway, but said nothing.

Noah took me home, evidently already prepared to stay the night. In tandem, we went through the motions of readying for bed, though it was only a bit after eight. Despite my leg, despite all the business with my pillows, I stayed the night on the sofa, with Noah's arms around me. A few times I slept.

When I woke the following morning, I was alone. Somehow Noah had managed to extricate himself without waking me. More shockingly, was the fact that he had woken up so easily.

"You must be worried about me," I said, entering the kitchen. He was cooking eggs at the stove.

"I am. Go on, these will be done in a few minutes."

I padded my way down the hall and back again a few minutes later.

"You don't have to worry." I picked up our conversation where I had left it.

He looked up from his breakfast with an expression that advertised what he thought of my claim.

"I wonder if things will be settled." He said, meaning no doubt the same things I had listed to myself last night, instead of counting sheep. Will Nick Morrison be arrested? Would he remain arrested? Who else held pieces of the puzzle that explained these events? Would the school survive this too?

"And I wonder if you will share with me what you are thinking." He looked at me across the table and I wished with all my heart that I could. But there were things I needed to learn before I could release this hold I had upon myself.

We arrived at school early, another shadow of earlier actions. I asked Noah to make the walk up the main path alone, since I was waiting for someone to find me. He did not look particularly happy, but went. I stopped by the bench where Dolores' papers had scattered. It was here that I first realized that secrets surrounded me like air.

"Why didn't you tell anyone?" I asked Sal Vacarro when he arrived.

"You knew Nick had already been here."

I was glad to have finally assigned a proper noun to this statement.

Sal was carrying another black garbage bag, this time clenched in his hands. I noticed how those hands were shaking when he sat next to me.

"I told you," he answered. "You figured it out. You see things, like Sister Paul."

I laughed mirthlessly at his assessment, still sickened at my blindness.

"Nick drank a lot. Here, all the time. I tried to help him, like Sister helped me."

I nodded, and thought of Bernadette accusing Sal of being a drunk. She had seen part of the truth but not paid attention to all of it. Sal no longer drank. But he clearly recalled his demons and recognized too much of Nick Morrison's frailty to expose him. He had waited for me to do it instead.

187

Rising, I turned to walk away, not wasting another glance behind me. I went onward to Sister Paul's office.

When Noah and I had arrived, I noticed two telling things about the parking lot. Dolores Donovan's car was not there and Ginny's was. I believed I had the answers to explain these facts but figured Sister could do it equally well. She had other answers to give me anyhow.

I was walking through the empty reception area when her voice beckoned. Ruefully I acknowledged I was still unaccustomed to the security cameras recording my every move. Given the events of the last day, I marveled that this could still be true.

Having a purpose made it easier to enter Sister's office, take my chair, and lead the conversation myself.

"Dolores knew Nick drank."

"Yes," Sister responded, quickly.

"She covered for him."

"Yes, as he covered for her when they were students, and Dolores caused the accident that debilitated Nick."

"More drinking."

"Yes." Sister sighed, and turned away from me for a moment. I thought she might stand up, perhaps go to the window to draw strength from the rising light, but she did not.

"Nick apparently confessed everything last night. I was speaking to Detective Lawson at four o'clock this morning."

I felt a moment's pity for the detective. He had doubtless not yet gone to bed at that hour, while Sister had already risen and said her morning prayers.

"He included running me over in his confession."

"Yes, Addra. He did." I thought I might have seen a tear glisten for a moment in Sister's eye, but again I was not sure. The shadows in this room were funny things.

When I had thought about what secret Tim could have held over Nick, I knew the drinking would have been enough. But my mind kept returning to Nick's new car, and the marks of the alley wall, and how Nick had changed since last year.

There were so many things we had all seen but not paid attention to. Adults like Mr. Delgado, Wanda and Mitch, Sister Paul, and myself. I wanted to believe Dolores and Coach Brown only had suspicions about Nick, and had not covered up his crimes. But I was unsure.

"We will have positions to fill?" I asked Sister calmly.

After staring at me for a moment, she answered.

"An athletic director, of course and a vice principal."

I watched her squirm a bit in her chair.

"We will be looking for a new football coach as well, after the season is over."

Like with Sal, I walked out without saying another word. Light was spilling from Dolores' office and I was sure I would find Ginny in there, unpacking her things.

Having learned a thing or two about strength, I got through the day. While I could not guarantee that the students were unaware of my turmoil, I did do my best to keep it at bay.

In class after class, I announced the quizzes I was slated to give tomorrow, being tired of surprises. A few of the seniors, Johnny Marchiano included, made a valiant effort to look aggrieved though they all knew it was coming.

Since people talk and I did not want to listen, I spent the day in my classroom, the door shut even while I was alone inside. By the last period bell I was starving and still undecided if I would even be coming to school tomorrow. Maybe I would just stay at home all day and bake pies, having given no thought to Saturday's fundraiser. Maybe I would go and sit in Mr. Delgado's living room, now that he had learned to turn on the lights.

Maybe I would ask Noah to ditch school too and we could spend the day together, talking about everything except this place.

I was still dreaming up possibilities when a bouquet of orange flowers walked into my room, followed by Johnny and Frankie.

"You always said orange was your favorite color," Frankie told me.

I smiled, since orange was my favorite color and because I could not recall ever having told him that. We do all pay attention sometimes, I reminded myself, hoping that it would be enough going forward.

"Thank you, gentlemen," I said, taking the flowers in my hand, where they looked much larger.

"You really are the best part of every day."

Noah walked in as I said that, giving Johnny and Frankie an opportunity to get away. They were boys after all, and the extent of their comfort around me had just been reached. But I imagined Frankie might have told me not to worry, since his mother no doubt cried at weird things too, just as often as she laughed at them.

"You'll take Ms. Lake somewhere nice?" Johnny asked Noah, while Frankie stood large at his side.

"I promise," Noah answered, looking at me.

And he did. He took me home.

Made in the USA
Lexington, KY
15 January 2014